ARAM PACHYAN

GOODBYE, BIRD

A NOVEL

Translated by Nairi Hakhverdi

Translation support was provided
by the Ministry of Culture of the Republic of Armenia

GLAGOSLAV PUBLICATIONS

GOODBYE, BIRD

A NOVEL

by Aram Pachyan

Translated by Nairi Hakhverdi

Book Cover and Interior Layout by Max Mendor

Translation support was provided
by the Ministry of Culture of the Republic of Armenia

Agreement by ARI Literary and Talent Agency

Glagoslav Publications Ltd
88-90 Hatton Garden
EC1N 8PN London
United Kingdom

www.glagoslav.com

ISBN: 978-1-911414-32-2

ARAM PACHYAN

GOODBYE, BIRD

A NOVEL

"Ich ruf zu dir, Herr Jesu Christ"

Johann Sebastian Bach

And I imagine that we are going
to set out the two of us alone
perhaps three and that no one
in the world will ever know
anything of our precious voyage toward
nothing but simply toward somewhere else and
forever
On this sea bluer still bluer
than any blue on earth
On this sea where no one would ever shout:
"Land!"[1]

Guillaume Apollinaire

---

[1] Guillaume Apollinaire, "Love, Disdain and Hope," in *Selected Writings: Guillaume Apollinaire,* trans. Roger Shattuck, New York: New Directions Books, 1971.

one

I am 28 years old. That's what it says at the beginning of every page in his notebook, which he opens up every hour, leafs through, and incessantly repeats that he is 28 years old, repeats it with his skin turning dark red with anxiety, first looking at his arms to check that two has not suddenly turned into three. Then he hangs his melon-looking head like the limp head of a dead man over one of the pages in his notebook and writes: two will never become three, because after being discharged the only governor of space and time is you, just like your grandfather who, at the break of dawn, finally closed the books on history. Look at how the 28-year-old Dürer depicts the savior's movement in his self-portrait! The mastery of improbable, mystifying brushstrokes. It's as if the brush worked from deep outer space with a guiding mix of the mind and the senses. The self-portrait of the 28-year-old Dürer is a creation challenging God to a duel; his time will always remain eternal, while you, who are already 28 years old, have no time left to yourself besides Bird. Absent-minded soldier. They're not embarrassed by the honesty of their own gaze and they don't kill the enemy from fear of shame. Not even a grain of soft honesty has remained in you to see time. SOFT honesty. At least make a promise to yourself now. Promise that you won't kill your dream from fear of shame. I promise that I will always be 28 and that I will not scratch up my face from fear of shame, and that every morning, until dawn, like my grandfather, I will eat a banana and drink a cup of coffee, feed Bird, bathe him, pet his fur, and at least once a month I will smoke Alejo's native tobacco and maybe one day, with a stroke of luck, like Schiele, I will catch some interesting 21st-century viral disease. He didn't know when his grandfather had eaten a banana for the first time–maybe it was while roofing in Russia or on the train that took orphans to Europe. But he remembers the day his grandfather lit his first cigar. That thin-veined brown cigar that moved the imagination seemed taller than his grandfather. He somehow jammed it between his lips, struck a match and brought it up to the tip of the cigar, all the while drilling him not to swallow the smoke. For one hour they took turns enjoying the cigar. They smoked and smiled. They smiled and smoked. Meanwhile, his grandfather elucidated the secrets of smoking cigars. He said that the chest should absolutely be puffed-out and that the lower lip should arrogantly droop down. Know that as long as this blue smoke is rising, you are a man standing nearest to God. He said this with a straight face and seeing his puffed-out chest and twitching lip, he suddenly chortled and laughed for a long, very long time. His grandfather's last friend, which was peeled strip by strip–his fingers feel the constraint, but they try to slow down so that he can live just a little longer, five more minutes, until he reaches the last morsel, which will be the most painful. The softness of the fleshy pulp will burn his throat and the drops of coffee will evaporate with a fizz. Then he will walk, he will walk out of the house to no longer walk and no longer return. Bravo, banana, you did not leave my grandfather's side. Bless your heart. There's silence in the office. I need to leave. It's as if my body is glued to the stiff chair. So leave without your body. There's knocking on the glass of the window. He turns around. It's the little banana. It's standing in front of the window, pressing its peel against the cold glass. It's pleading. Come on, come, you're running late, they're waiting for you. I'm coming. On the desk. My desk has the color of pomegranates and is strewn with a letter of resignation, a notebook, a pen, and shredded pieces of my girlfriend's photograph. He slowly collects his possessions. He crams his notebook and pen into the sack-like bag hanging from his chair, then he crouches under the table and somewhat shyly puts the shredded pieces of the photograph one by one into his mouth, working, as he chews, on softly grinding his molars. My crazy kitten, today at noon, as I was saying goodbye to the office, I ate one half of a half of you, then the other half, chewing our memories with care so that they would be digested easily. Let your body live inside of me. Walk with me. Tingle all over. Flutter with delight. I've made up my mind. I'm going. There's no time. He crouches. He goes under the chair on all fours. He shoves the rest of the pens and pencils he took from the desk under the carpet. He kisses and licks the fuzzy little tassels of the carpet. Forgive me, my friend, please, forgive me for everything, I didn't want to hit you, I burned your beautiful face for those dirty plates. You went and shot straight into your mouth. Does one feel the taste of bullets in one's mouth? A current of air ripples the tassels of the carpet like grass. He gets up. He throws his bag over his shoulder. He sadly looks at his fur coat and scarf swaying on the coat rack. He puts on his fur coat and wraps himself with the scarf you gave him. Which shop in Paris did you get it from? The shop is probably called "Blue Peace" or "Crocodile Heart." Lying in bed at night, he imagines the display windows of the shop and the saleswoman whose face looked like it had been scratched up with the tip of a thick nail. From one of the shops in Paris, you picked out a scarf for me, a s c a r f, with your delicate fingers. In the dark, it's as if the word flies out of your mouth. It has entered my mouth, it has opened my mouth, and with my mouth it is drawing the scarf that was knitted in another country and exudes the maddening scent of your skin. The excitement makes the palms of your hands sweat. Thump, th-thump, thump, thump. The heart. Courage is needed to listen to the beats of the heart in the dark. You want to drink. He reaches under the bed. His fingers rub against Bird's whiskers. He gently strokes the nose of the cat for a long time, then he somehow finds the bottle, picks it up, puts it to his mouth, and, contracting the muscles in his face, slowly chugs it down. Your fingers rest on my shoulder blades, because I sleep on my stomach to begin our dialogue, and very often I pretend, like you, to be sleeping so that you hold my back with your gentle hand, so that your lips lightly press on my shoulder and quiver with your dreamy breathing. Sky-blue lip lines turned dark red with excitement. Your tongue glides over the edges of your lips, wetting the dry heat. Hold the tip of your tongue with your teeth and thrust it into my mouth. To steal your tongue, to take it between my lips, to feel its sharp presence. One strap of your black bra has slipped down your shoulder and fallen on your thin sparkling gold fuzzy arm. You rub against the strap of her bra with your nose and lightly nibble her arm with a quaver. Don't you wake up, don't you come out of that sweet slumber. I don't want to hurt you with my shameless presses, but I know that you're not sleeping, because your cheek slowly caresses the pillow softly. You wait for my nightly surprise attacks, you wait with crafty hints. Suddenly you envelop my back with your legs, pull your short nightgown to your hips and roll like a cat, embracing my body. The warm current that flows between your legs burns my thighs. And I dream that any minute now you will simply take off your nightgown, that any minute now you will finally remove from your body that final silky gauze that separates us, and you know that I'm waiting for you to suddenly kiss my neck around dawn in your wakeful sleep, for your tongue to stick out through your lips and prick my skin like a little fish nose, and for everything to start all over again under the first droplets of sun shining through the window. But you continue to rub against the corner of the pillow. Her shiny black nipple, covered with tiny little glands, whose tip you gently hold between your incisors and stroke with your tongue, massaging it endlessly. The heat of your palate fills her breast. She's moaning intensely, digging her fingers in your hair, and pressing your head down with her other hand, she pushes her breast deeper into your mouth. The room becomes permeated with the semi-sweet scent of your naked and lone bodies. It was only inside of her that you could forget about your presence; it was inside of her that you could make your own body disappear; it was through her kindness and moisture that you could come to yourself. Irises swallowed by the whites of the eyes. They already sparkle on the distant horizon. Deep, deep penetration. The throbbing of pleasant pain. With sweet thrusts. It penetrated deeply, so deeply that there was a new beginning after that, a new space, a new meaning, so deeply that for a moment happiness was almost attainable, palpable and found, so deeply that death and separation seemed unattainable then. There was as much silence inside of him as there was inside of a house that had been abandoned a long time ago. You would succumb to the craze of return and that escape was her only light, which was surrendered to you as a last chance, a willful surrendering pull, a confession not uttered in a long time. You leave the bed. She sits on the carpet. You stand over her head and look at the dark cleavage separating her breasts. She starts to move her breasts with her palms, back and forth, taking long breaks. She squeezes them. She pushes them together. And you have bent over almost breathlessly, you are stroking her shady hair draped over her shoulder blades with your mouth and cheeks, carefully, trying not to touch her skin, and then you hold her back, and then you kiss her fragile shoulders, and then you lie on your back, and then she comes to you, very slowly, slowly; slowly; your expectation is so impatient that your skin tingles, and she knows that you can never bear it and she uses it to her advantage, turning seconds into centuries, her nipples sticking out before her breasts, which descend down the back of your neck, drawing singular lines with their tips all the way to the end of your median furrow, and ascend again. You feel the breasts entering your body, and they like each of the layers of your body, then the breasts move through you, break open your rib cage, and burst out. Now you can feel her breasts on your body, you can feel her hips, her groin, her thighs, her knees, her lips, the ankles of her feet, the thin, thin veins going through her ankles.

You probably walked down Flaubert's streets in Paris and felt my impatient and wet tongue play from your neck to your mouth. Now I've wrapped the scarf you gave me around my throat, and with my bag over my shoulder I stand frozen between the desks: tell me, what should I do? I don't know, but you have a colleague you're not saying goodbye to. You hate that person. His haircut. The way he sits. His accent. The artificial hiss under his breath every five minutes. His everyday presence. For a moment today, you wonder what the mole on your cheek looks like from where he's sitting: does it look big or small? Does he cast a brief glance at your face? What does he think of the pocks on your cheeks? Will he know that those are leftover traces from chickenpox? Chickenpox. The end of a daydream. Little green dots. The sun is a little green dot. Each one has its own character. No little green dot feels pain the same way. At night they itch like crazy. I want to scratch my skin off with my nails. My mother hugs me. Where did you get that much strength from? You've turned into a skeleton. You're tired of waiting for your husband. Don't give yourself hope, the war will go on for a long time, and you, you coward, you don't have the courage to betray your husband. You forgot to wash your hands. The smell of spilled oil from the pipes of the heater wafts from your fingers. Jeans-wearing woman quickly tapping heater pipes. Are you playing mother? Under the flickering light of the lamp you resemble an old sallow woman. Your skin hangs from your cheeks like the withered skin of a peach. You're holding me in your arms. My temple is leaning against your rib cage where once upon a time one could feel two triangular breasts for which you can no longer find fitting bras. You push the balcony door with your foot. We get out into the clean air. You somehow stop me. Lean against the balcony balustrade. You say, look at how pretty the lights of the street lanterns are. You stand behind me and blow with all your might so that my burning back cools down a little– whoooooooooooosh, whoooooooooooosh, the burn intensifies. I can't take it anymore. I try to get on the balcony balustrade. Throw myself down. You grab my sides terrified, you pull me towards you and hold me tight. Let go of me! How beautifully the light that flows out of the little lanterns ripples! I want to catch the movements in the air with my mouth. Dense green suns, one by one stamped on my face with care. You're not leaving. You have fallen asleep next to me. Coward. Who told you to get pregnant and warm up your protruding belly in the sun every day? Now you're not sleeping. I know. You've supposedly closed your eyes. For show. You gave birth to me with your eyes closed out of fear; chicken's pox. Instead of preventing the doctor from slapping my behind, you were howling in labor pains. At least the doctor slapped fair and square, without gloves. And my first word, without anyone asking me, without my permission, was a terrifying screech born from the pain of the slap that had been given me. Two little dots on my eyelids; the tips of my lashes are steeped in green algae; green world.

Bird has jumped on the bed and is lying at my feet meowing restlessly. He takes a burning cigarette out of his mouth and tries to put it in the cat's mouth. It turns its head. It doesn't want it. Then he puts his hand under the bed again. There should be another bottle. Suddenly his fingers rub against a familiar and disgusting bald spot. It's impossible. My God. It's the commander again. He shakes his body and tries to call for help, and through the half-open door of his room he sees the contortions of his own terrified face, his mute mouth opening and closing in weightlessness, and his mouth's resilient movements in a vacuum. Drops of cognac slowly flow down the edges of his lips. He tries to strain his consciousness, tries to understand whether anyone in the house can hear that terrifying screech leaving his throat or whether it's him, only him who can hear his own screech. The commander breathes steadily. The air blowing out of his nostrils burns. I've been discharged for a while now, you hear? Leave me alone, commander! What do you want, you son of a bitch? Every night you come and hide under my bed and scatter my brain with the chain in your hand. But your chain doesn't hurt me anymore. Flog the corpse as much as you want. I neither have flesh nor blood. Are you that stupid, you still don't get it, you deformed miscarriage? Don't you understand that your beatings now are completely meaningless? You're nothing outside of the military base, you one-legged scarecrow planted in a field! Impotent. Back then, in your room, you hit me so much that the skin on my face, my nose, my mouth, my chin shattered, then you made me sweep up every piece of my face one by one, and splitting your sides with laughter, you said, take it to the open window and let the wind carry it away. You bequeathed me an eternal pastime after my discharge, commander! Now I stand by the window all day looking out for hours and I make up facial features in the rising wind that turn into sharp shards, glide away, and get lost in a cloud of dust. But, do you remember, commander, how you scratched up my face with your teeth? You turned everything on its head. The boys were saying that you supposedly sharpened your row of gold teeth with an electric sharpener every morning. They were probably joking or maybe they were telling the truth. I didn't feel any pain, commander, it's just that the more you hit my head, the deeper my inner emptiness and sadness grew. Every hit on my head taught me how to think, taught me how to remember again and go, leaving my body behind under your shoes. He tightly closes his mouth with both hands. He clenches his teeth and presses his fingers together so that through no crack, through no narrow passage, your spit, your disgusting spit, will bound into my mouth. During the morning formation, in the motionless silence, I couldn't hold in my friend's wonderful mime jokes and I chuckled, and I didn't know that for laughing I would have to pay with my mouth for two years, I didn't know that my laugh would be my mouth's last goodbye. When you dragged me into your room, closed the door, and started to break my body with dull and rhythmic strikes, at that moment the strikes seemed so real to me, so angry and blunt that I experienced them as an important acquisition to what had been missing from my body all these years–as an honest flattery. But you moved to my mouth. My mouth was what you needed. You laughed with this trap, didn't you, birth of a whore? This is the trap you couldn't shut, wasn't it, soldier? Now watch me shut it! I have to fight for you, lay down my life, hold up a homeland for a motherfucker like you, so that you can't control your trap? Foaming stream with popping white bubbles. Slowly, very slowly, from your blood-gushing cheeks, which will later glitter in a sad wooden box in the middle of your living room like a little isle veiled with makeup. You couldn't hold your laugh during the morning formation. Your friend Zizu's face contorted and changed with such improbable flexibility into different moods and conditions that not laughing would simply equal to not breathing. The commander holds your throat with one hand and with the fingers of the other hand he squeezes your jaw, trying to open your mouth. The pressure of his fingers makes the corners of your lips crack open. Your mouth opens up. You move your head from side to side, shaking uncontrollably. You are struck against the floor with your temple and the top of your forehead. The commander gathers up a good swill of saliva and spits straight into your mouth. Suddenly you start to laugh, laugh, laugh hysterically with cackles and snorts. Your chest thunders and your legs point straight up into the air. Somehow confused by the surprise, the commander grabs you by the hair and starts to beat your head against the floor. Your laugh becomes even more intense. The dull and inescapable roar thudding against the walls of the room is reborn. The commander starts to erratically sputter in your face. Then he closes your mouth with the palm of his hand. Shut up, asshole, shut up! Are you trying to call the cops on me? You want me to kill you, is that what you want? His palm has embalmed your mouth. Now your laugh fills up inside. It finds its own way. It goes to a place you've never been. It laughs for silence, modestly rejoicing at itself. Before going to the army, your mother would tell you what a beautiful soldier you'd make. Now she won't even look at my face. We speak with our shoulders. I stand in front of the mirror for hours and comb my hair with a little comb, my hair is not visible, or, more precisely, I don't see myself, I positively realize that I don't see. I don't exist and I realize the realization that I don't exist, it seems as if I have existed and I do exist, but you can't see that I have existed and I do exist, it seems as if it's the comb that's grooming my hair, but without a comb and without hair. I point my finger at the mirror where a young man stands, but without a finger and without a young man–I'm simply a blind spot. Shame on you, you little whore. You've dragged your heavy stars, you've come after a dead man. Why did you come? What do you want? Do you have amnesia? And now you come after your discharged soldiers? Did you open a corpse factory? I'm looking for a job, if there's a vacancy, I'd love to work there. But why do you slither every day and lie under my bed? Doesn't your wife like you either? I know, you're one of those tough old boys used to fields and soil, facing your face up to space. Don't you have a home and a wife, don't you have soldiers to violate anymore? What do you want from me? I already know where you live and I quit my job, because I've already saved up all my money for a gun, beeeeeeeee caaaaaaaaaareful veeeeeeeeeery caaaaaaaaaareful, commander, IIIIIIIIIII will shooooooooooooooooot straight into your forehead, I'm not afraaaaaaaaaaaaaaaid. I keep a knife under my pillow now. I'm serious. I'll turn on the light and cut your throat or call my mother. You don't know my mother very well. If she comes, she'll kick the life out of you, and don't you ever touch Bird again. You hear? Bird is not one of the boys you knew. It doesn't have a mouth. Instead of coming and making coffee even just once and talking about our service, the military tactics of the enemy, the fate of the army, your glorious past, I think you've accomplished quite a few heroic feats, no, or did you make those up? Well, whatever, even if you were making things up, that's okay, we all make things up. The measure of things made-up is never excessive. His sheets are drenched and clinging to his body. The big drops of sweat quiver on the apples of his cheeks. He picks up the cat and tightly presses it against his chest. Bird is not a soldier, you whore. You won't slaughter it anymore, you won't catch it under the wall of the mess hall and you won't break its neck, and you won't hurl its head at our feet. It's all the same, we won't tell you whose cat it is. Asshole, "whose is it?" never relates to a cat. It was the unit's cat whose head you tore off. The fur by its neck was torn. Its coagulated blood had stuck to its fur like a little tick. It wasn't breathing. You shouldn't kill a cat, commander. It's a sin. I know, I read it somewhere. The ancient Egyptians cursed those who raised their hand against a cat, they subjected them to terrible tortures. Cats are friends to humans. They cure many diseases. They cure everybody, even babies born sick. The babies are born sick–they're born, they feel pain and then they die. But suddenly one day between life and death they suddenly see a cat in the window and they extend their plump little hands towards it. Their little cheeks tremble in joy and their irises sparkle as sparks of being alive. You, too, have extended your finger towards a cat and your finger was also plump, but at that time they had lied to you. At the military base, we did not eat cat meat. We preferred dog. Don't laugh, the Egyptians won't forgive you. I've asked those old boys. Whoever kills cats falls into their world. The cats enter your body and then they meow, they constantly meow. They don't kill you, they don't bite your lungs, your kidneys, your windpipe, because you fall into their world gutted, so that it's spacious for them inside. They only meow and meow and meow. The cats have made you immortal so that you hear their meows forever, so that you're the only one who hears their echoes. They say that cats meow to forget their own nightmares. There's no escape from consciousness. You try to die from the terror. No, it's not working. You have no strength. You cat-filled bag, meeeeeeeeeeeeeeeeeeoooooooo oooooooooow meeeeeeee meeeeeeeeeeeeeeeeeeeooooooooooooooo ooooow what are you staring at, commander? Are you trying to remember my name? Anonymous cadet. Remember? To leave the room I now have to empty the whole bottle of cognac and find courage again, open the door and scurry out. He empties the bottle to the last drop. He holds Bird and keeping his balance somehow he opens the heavy door. Now you have to start walking, little soldier. Don't be afraid. Walking will distance you. Lift your foot. Put it on the floor or on the window sill. But make sure to look at the traffic on the street first. Make sure there aren't any children on the street. They'll get very scared. They don't have to see. Lovely children with gentle smiles and soft hands. It'll probably rain outside. Fine, if you want, let it rain. And to get to the marketplace you have to keep walking down the street. You're right, to get somewhere you always have to walk. So here we go, don't forget to move your feet first. The bus full of conscripts is waiting for you. Your family waves goodbye. You see that moment a few times. You're standing in front of the bus doors with a waxed bag in your hand. How wretched and weak the waxed bag in your hand looks! I don't understand, wasn't there another bag in the house? Your mother's, sister's, grandfather's... their faces are stuck to your face. They're breathing straight into your mouth. They move their hands back and forth and slap your cheeks with all their might. Why are they slapping you, why can't they kiss your cheeks at least, instead of painfully slapping them? They've pressed their faces firmly on my face. It'd be better if they entered my mouth. I'm still confident that my mouth is the safest place, that no one in the military unit will find out that I hide my family in my mouth. When everyone is fast asleep at night, I'll take them out, I'll line them up on the blue camouflage bedding of my mesh base bed and I'll share my thoughts with them, and then we'll play war games together like little tin soldiers, and at dawn I will put them back in my mouth. I'll hide them. Eeeeeeeeh, hurry up, soldier, you're not expecting us to wait for you for hours, are you? Say goodbye and be done. You're no longer a part of the outside world. Hurry up, say goodbye. The short lieutenant with crooked legs squealed like a pig annoyed at the heat. Dumbstruck waxed bag: sad and swaying in front of the open doors of the bus. Am I not talking to you? Are you not listening? Say something, too, sad swaying waxed bag. The engine of the bus starts with a sputter. Burning throat. A bag swaying in a kind breeze: the neck did not ward off the rope. The powerful kick of the lieutenant's half-shoe on your back throws your body to the ground. Fall in! Foooorward, march! One, one, one, two, three, left, left, left, right, left

He's trying to trample the leaves that have fallen to the ground on the street, he's walking down the familiar road, free, with his eyes closed, as if it were the hallway in his house that leads from the bathroom to the bedroom. You are led by shop signs, by pediments of nearby buildings, by open balconies, by half-wet whites hanging from clotheslines, by rippling window glass, by sheer valance curtains, by chandeliers oscillating from ceilings and flickering shadows, by traces in windows of hideous old women's cheekbones, by waxing and waning silhouettes of unfamiliar women. Your face contorts at some uncertain anxiety. You're sweating. You're breathing heavily. Your mouth is parched. You walk up to a newsstand and ask the saleswoman for a glass of water. Staring through the little window, she extends a yellow glass filled with water. You drink slowly, one gulp after another, looking restlessly around you. With your head down, you return the glass through the little window. The saleswoman takes it, then extends her hand once more through the window and suddenly digs her fingers in your hair and gently strokes your hair with the weak movements of her fingers and the tips of her nails. Gentle fingers, moving joints that hardly quiver under thin skin, your nails, painted dark red, dig into my hair, stroke the back of my neck, with both arms you hold my back, the more I pressed down your body, the deeper you dug your nails into my skin, and I could see the movement of your fingers with nails painted with dark red polish stroking my back, I could see it pressed against the ceiling of the room as if I were separating from my body, examining your half-closed eyes from a little distance, your cheek pressed against my cheek, my lips kissing your shoulder, a pale face turned to the ceiling, the blondeness of locks mixed with shadows, then the light of the street lanterns shining through the window flickering under the soles of your feet walking over my back, whose cold, pleasant presses slowly moved over my spine to my nape, weightless, bare feet–soft steps, feathery– you've opened your hands like the wings of an aeroplane, and somehow keeping the balance of your body, you walk over my back, counting out loud: ooooooooooooone, twooooooooooooo, threeeeeeeeeeee, and near the back of my neck you suddenly crash down on my back, turn my head around, and kiss deeply. Through your parted lips, the tip of your naughty tongue discernible in the dark shadow comes to prod itself into my mouth, probe around, and demolish my insides. Waited for two years for the naughty tongue discernible in the dark shadow through your parted lips, got discharged, waited, and did not find it. The dark red nail polish paints your nails to dig into someone else's skin. At least don't use my favorite dark red nail polish. At least change the color in my memory. Is everything okay? Nothing happened, huh? Are you not feeling well? No, I'm walking. I've just started getting tired faster. Okay, then go, only look under your feet when you walk and don't suddenly raise your head or they'll notice you. He draws down the window and leaves the depths of the newsstand. A street with gray sidewalks leading to a fruit market; the neon cross of a pharmacy with a green flickering snake coiled around it; the egg-shaped, whiskey-colored perfume vials; the loud din coming out of pizzerias. As you walk, they are imprinted in your memory as dim, transitory shimmers of colors, subjects, sensations, and sounds. One day, when you're passing time in bed, they will become images, like a little baby playing with the toy hanging from his crib with his hand, all alone in the silence of the dark room. As you cross the intersection, you suddenly freeze, unexpectedly turn around and look at me, then you avert your gaze, as if you were looking in another direction all along and you count the leaves trampled under your feet again: one, two, three, three, wait a second, four, five, six. Listen, do you remember the giant oak tree by the office under which it's very probable there are fallen leaves? Let's go crush them. Wait, let me think a little. You're barely able to stop yourself. You'd really like to turn around and crush all of the leaves under the oak tree, but it's late. I'm sorry, I can't come. You go, I have people waiting for me. You continue to walk, pushing your hands into your pants pockets. You touch two sunflower seeds in one of them. There was only supposed to be one seed. Where did the second one come from? The first one was there from last week. You had bought it at the beach for 20 drams. The seller was a little fisher boy with a giant hump on his back. He had covered one of his eyes with a black patch and tied a toy truck to his foot. He was a real pirate.

That day, instead of going to the office, you picked up Bird, bought two bottles of whiskey, grabbed your bag, sat on the number 72 yellow bus from the bus stop on Babayan Street, got off at the last stop, and walked for an hour over blackish, gloomy stones until you reached the beach. In the mottled morning mist that has still not lifted, you and Bird have frozen side by side on this deserted shore. Both of you are looking. You gulp down the strong whiskey, mixing it with a mouthful of tiny pebbles and slimy shells, which are not chewed properly because of the weak movements of your jaws. The little pirate walks up unnoticeably. He suddenly pops up in front of you, tightly holding a fishing rod in his hand. It's the first time in your life that you see a fishing rod that small for catching fish. It's the size of a pen. Hands up, the boy says, holding the rod to your forehead. I'm the world's most evil pirate. They call me one-legged, one-eyed Bear. I aaaaaaaaam aaaaaaaaas strong aaaaaaaaas a Bear, because IIIIII caaaaaaaaan hit. He presses the rod against your forehead. His little hand shakes a little. Who gave you permission to look at my sea, eh? To hide your inebriation from the child, you try to avoid looking into his eyes, you stroke Bird's back, which is purring and sniffling and rubbing its tail against Bear's leg. I'm sorry, one-legged, one-eyed Bear, I'll leave now. But Bear suddenly steps back, the rod in his hand loosens and slips down your forehead. Bear crouches down before you, lowers his head and, finding your downcast eyes, he looks at you with a pitiful gaze. The sea waves in his irises bring to mind sparkling boats on the horizon, and the sea is so sad in the child's eyes. Deep down he probably doesn't want you to leave. Well, fine, I won't hit you. It's sad. Is this your cat? Watch me kill it. Bear jumps back on his feet, erratically sticks the rod up in the air, and angrily looks at the cat. Psht. Run, moron. Psht. Unfazed, Bird squints and casts such an indifferent glance at the rod erratically sticking up in the air and another glance at Bear's angry face, then sprawls again on the stones. It's not afraid? You don't say a word, and with your index finger you play with the fuzzy brown moss covering the round pebble. If your cat died, would you be very sad? Your voice is smothered by the thunder of giant waves crashing against the cliffs. Fine, I'll let you look at my sea, but on one condition, you have to buy the fish I caught, you hear, let's go, I'll show you,–the boy says, pointing his finger in an unclear direction, then pulling twice on your wiry hair with his little thumb and index finger, he walks. You pick up the bottle and bag and silently follow the excited little boy's short and angry steps. Bird walks next to you meowing. Clunk, clunk, clunk, clunk–almost half of the truck tied to his foot has fallen apart from crashing against stones. Some time later he suddenly stops in his tracks and opens up his arms wide as a bird's. This is it. We're here. Don't move. You're standing in a thick feather of mist, as if on a swaying carpet. You're barely able to see any-thing. You feel little mounds and large beachrocks under your feet. He bends over and beckons you. You slowly walk up to him and crouch next to him. Bear lifts up an egg-shaped beachrock and points at a barely visible sunflower seed in the brittle sand. Have you ever seen a fish like this in your life, with five eyes and blue feathers? It doesn't even have a heart. He's glowing with happiness. His cheeks are blushing. No, I've nev-er seen one. See? I was after it for ten days and I barely caught it near Africa. And my boat got a hole in it, so I brought it here without a boat. Well now, pay up and take the fish. You slip your hand into your pocket, take out two ten-dram coins, and hand them over to the boy. He looks at the money obviously disappointed. You're this poor? They beat you every day and tell you, go to the beach and collect money from people, yeah? If you don't collect any, you won't get anything to eat in the evening, huh? You won't be allowed into your house? You've cast your head down. You don't have anymore money? Really, could it be that you're a beggar? Your dad, your mom, do they beat you? I'm sorry, Bear, I don't have anymore money. Okay fine, fine, don't cry. Give me the money. He takes the two ten-dram coins from the palm of your hand, restlessly puts them in his pants pocket, and carefully puts the sunflower seed in the palm of your hand, then turns around suddenly and romps off, clunk, clunk, clunk, clunk, he endlessly turns around and laughs, then he disappears completely in the gliding fog, and one can only hear his presence-betraying laugh. One second, Bear. Stop. You run after him, penetrating the blue-veined milky fog. You slip over slippery pebbles, falling and getting up. Bear laughs and laughs. You strain your hearing and try to hunt down the trail of his laugh, to run after the non-imprint-ed traces of his laugh. Suddenly you stop, feeling a sharp pain in your elbow and a flowing warmth. But again you run after his fleeting laugh. Beeeeeeeeeeaaaaaaaaaaaar. Stop. Your legs feel heavier. You look down. You're up to your knees in icy water. Suddenly the fog completely rips apart. The endless sea is before you. The gray waves form a line of giant gates. The masses of the rolling water oppress the sky. The peaks of the waves curl with horrifying sounds, the white bubbles heave and turn, dissolving with pops in the melding ashy clearing. The sound of the sea swallows up Bear's ringing laugh. Now it's as if the waves are laughing, out-of-reach, sad, and forever moving away. Your presence has made the sea even more emotional. It rumbles in your soul. *Why does it never exist and is always* *present?*2 Jays are flying about, lolling on the peaks of waves like white balloons dancing in the wind, expanding the sad space of the sky. You sit in the icy water. Your body feels numb. You somehow swig down the last drops of whiskey. Beeeeeeeeeeeeeeeeeeeeaaaaaaaaaaaaaaaaaaaaaaaaaar. The tall waves reach your body, hurl you to the ground, and cover you. The sandy water fills in your mouth and goes down your throat. Gurgling and suffocating, you try to throw up some of it. Your mouth has a hard time closing. Your lips have torn open. They're terribly swollen. Your orange drivel flows from the corners of your mouth. The wave comes again, crashing. You only manage to close your mouth and hold your breath. Bird's meowing is audible through some distant wind, as if it were coming from the depths of some imageless dream. How quiet it is beneath the wave, how safe and lonely; like beneath eternal masses of ice where the sounds of dinosaurs have long fallen silent, like in your mother's womb where you rock like a rickety rowboat. Don't come up to inhale life's gruesome thoughts on death, to ask questions, and to search for answers. The ruling mother of whys, together with the searchers of whys, all of them have ripped apart unripped. Twenty-eight years old, meandering degenerate, relic like all ancients, supposedly not conforming to the present, many relics like you will still come and go, leaving aside the sea's moving beauty, which is the only tangible image; the sea has no now and then, it does not feel the weight of your body on its shore, where you now lie, millions of years ago, herbivorous, long-necked, dinosaurs grazed with kind smiles, and hirsute mammoths sprayed the sea's water over their bodies with their elongated trunks, there has

---

2   From Kostan Zarian, *United States*

been no before you and no after you, through the vast waters, *in my end is my beginning.*3 Now the waves stroke your body like your soft blanket that became even softer especially on New Year's Eve, when your father and mother put a toy car and beautiful shiny mask under your pillow and pulled, holding onto the corners of your pillow, to cover your bare shoulders, there's no difference at all, just that modeling clay has been exchanged for a blend of blood-flesh-bones; bed leaning against the bedroom wall, a ray of moon reflecting through the window that glides over his little nose and his sensitive lips that quaver from a dream; the room has filled with tiny lungs the size of buttons that exhale the sweet milky scent of sleep; poking out from under the covers, a small child's innocent shoulders on which, it happens, there are beautiful birthmarks or flecks–all shoulders have had a sensation of feeling gifts being put under their pillow on New Year's Eve and of their shoulders being covered with a soft blanket, I know, they have; turning and folding water wrinkles, a couple of loose silky threads, fluttering coffin shroud brushing against your deathly pale frizzy hair, and your mother's fingers softly stroking your frizzy hair, the tips of her nails now and then brushing against the fluttering shroud and the coffin's shiny polish, plucker of fruit from grandpa's tree, its zealous conscience that singles out fruits to be plucked from the branches one by one, no, it had no conscience, because the overripe fruits neighed in terror at being eaten and plucked, but there was happiness, there was a little girl's screech in the suspensions of the leaves and branches, the orchard was evil, but it was old and had the good gaze of a wine-drunk man, while his movement was like flesh pulled

---

3   From T.S. Eliot, "Four Quartets."

down to the bone and, on the bone, braids and groups of muscles, then blood, as if someone has poured zest from the wine decanter into rivers called veins, in Karin, hands of masters built carriage wheels, knobby lumps on theirs fingers, warts, crystallized on the inside, knuckles covered in calluses with the gloomy, skin-tearing roughness of branches, but it was gentle, gentle, it shaved down the wood ferociously, but the pulp and the splinters gently, with an almost impalpable smoothness, like the dream of your hand caressing a girl's skin, sliding from one curve to another, sliding and letting the softness make the heart pound; the popping crackles of fire in the quiet of the night, the wheel singes the orange tongues with every turn, the firmness of that rough hand carving wheels of eternity, that rough callused carving hand pouring sand down your nape as you sit under trees grown under the weight of the sun as mirrors of the sun, the rustling leaves betray the ferity of grandfather's short steps, his fierce hand, which had wrapped three knots around the rope so that goddamn death would not suddenly seize him from life; one hand, one rope, one stumble, a stump under your feet, the shadows of trees on shaved and clean ruddy cheeks, a small dark spot on the edge of your lips, they received an order in Karin from Paris for carriage wheels, I know, the most amazing wheels were prepared for Gustave Flaubert and his lover Louise Colet, who were then going to play Bovary and Leon, and those amazing wheels roll through the streets of Paris by Saint-Sever, the Quai des Curandiers, the Quai aux Meules, the Place du Champ de Mars, behind the hospital gardens, they saw it, they see it at La Rouge-Marc, at Place du Gaillardbois, then they see in on Papazian, on Aram Khachatryan, it goes down on Komitas, enters Sayat-Nova through Baghramyan, turns onto Teryan, goes down, goes down, sir, what is your final destination? wherever you want, the familiar voice rings from an intangible distance; they see the shadow of the carriage in the narrow streets of the Cascade, they see it coming down Abovyan, suddenly near the Puppet Theater, in front of the Chess House, at the hard-to-cross intersection of Kond, gliding by "Kostan Zaryan" books and little bow tie shop windows; without stopping, the carriage goes on until dawn, feeling the moist non-dewiness of alleys, the cobblestones, the wheels' obstinate but smooth turns; grandfather's hand that cut ornamental carvings on the wheels, that upon seeing me in the courtyard in the morning dug into my hair like a pickaxe, rumpling my hair, and asked, are you okay? You look sad, did something happen? And you get greedy, you shake your head like a lunatic, you glide into the forest and roam around until late in the night, feeling all day on the surface of your head his heavy right, how much bottled-up noise there was in the silence of his hand, how many shadows of trees there were and waters, which streamed after work, washed the length of his arms, even if you shaved your hair, the trace won't vanish, the weight of his five fingers, like flowing thick black earth, is one feisty man, you take one handful of black earth, it's a man, or the eye of a fallen soldier by a sniper rifle, or the small bun on the back of a girl's neck, or a bird, or the scut of a rabbit, well now, a handful of earth is human and that's what's important; no one else besides your grandfather in the mornings has asked you whether you're okay, no one else has come to terms with your piggish personality, your innately evil inclinations, your tendency to sullenly torture everyone for pleasure, your genuine disgust for your mother and father, your endless deceptions; centimeter by centimeter, to not die in the winter, branches were cut from the trees in the forest, which were turned into brooms, made and sold with the little boy's little hand, which was familiar, which was a familiarity, it was somehow necessary for you, it was a comforting moment; contractions of muscle tendons that stroked your head shamelessly bridled the horse-woman; no one, except for that hand, has accepted you the way you are, they accepted you the way you are not, they provoked you into deception and subservience right from the start, they tried to distract you from how you were made, they forced you to become good, they forced it, but they never showed you, they lied to you that you are the best, while you are the worst, which is your truth; they taught you not to blame, that is not to blame disability, they taught you to work and work, work and work, work, work, so that your life becomes a savage and numb immobility; you are a total egoist, because you only value that one hand that stroked your head, with the savage honesty of a prehistoric man, without the haughty voice of the tree, that asked in the morning, are you okay? You get up on the stump, rolling on the deserted shore of the sea, rolling from the tall waves, now rolling on the sand, now rocking on the peak of the waves. Bird is happily playing with the stump. The hair on its back rises with a hiss, it freezes under the stump and waits. He hits it hard out of fear with a trembling paw and hysterically hops around trying to push it back.

Through a net of sand grains filled in your eye sockets, you see with half-opened eyes. You're face-down on the ground. You no longer have anything to drink, the bottle's not there anymore–it's probably voyaging through the open sea. The sand grains rasp in your mouth. Let the waves lick all of you, and you watch how he barely rises like rolling and folding shadows, whimpering in pain and emptiness, he clenches his teeth and holds his cat, then stands for a long time, undecided, gazing at the tears in his pants around his knees, then he leaves, feeling disgust at the sullen hollowness of the stones, and with wretched, crude steps, he somehow reaches the bus stop. The pack of cigarettes is lost in the water. He pulls a crumpled smoke out of the pack and puts it in his mouth. He can't find a lighter. The doors of the yellow number 72 bus soon open right under his nose. How to conquer these few black steps? The yellow bus will take him to a place where they speak in whispers. He strolls with half-closed eyes from where he's standing. Bird has fallen asleep on his lap. He sees a strange man waiting at the bus stop who's having trouble walking and decides to help him by letting him lean on his arm, lifting him over the steps one by one, carefully seating him in a seat, and putting his hand on his shoulder, asks somewhat shyly whether he should call emergency. If you don't feel well, I'll call now. Every day in the morning when you'd leave your house and enter the people-filled street, you always thought that there must be someone in the crowd who, if need be, would call emergency, and you thought about the life of the emergency-calling person, which is most mystifying. You don't know why you're convinced that that life is outside of all life, that it's insignificant, a sort of unimportant solitude-loving self-satisfaction. That person probably also loves dogs. He has put his hand with such care and respect on your shoulder, it's as if he doesn't want the pressure to cause even the slightest annoyance or pain. No, thank you, I just want to lean my head against the cold window; lean against the cold glass of the window and feel my return to her, because you aaaaaare sleeeeeeeping ooooooh craaaaaaaaazy giiiiiiiiiirl, and I'm returning from the military base, my return is your body's memory, while your body is my return's desire, and I am stroking your naked shoulder sketched in the flooding light, sliding under your blouse with a breeze in the flooding light, caressing and rubbing your skin, recognizing her entire breathing and maddening fragrance that soaks up my numb existence like dawn's hidden shadows, shines through me, pours out or explodes inside of me, embracing our past and future, all of our unembraced days, while you curl up your gentle shoulder even more, and I, in the milky mist, suddenly hunt down your curling movement's soft wave that ripples across your breast; your skin tingles, surprised at the touch of my lips, at the slow excavations of my awaited lips in your curves, which are simply imperceptible, indomitable to our consciousness; my slender girl, I've returned right at this moment and I'm standing in front of you; I'm looking again at your bra's thin, black strap, which in the light is simply a black flit, a bent trail; this is the path of final return, and I am walking over your bra's thin, black strap, I'm walking without looking back, without responding to the commander's threatening commands, just like a mute leaf spinning in the wind; I'm coming, with skulking courage, because I know that you're my last salvation, my last word; I've come to love your body, to enter it, to remember and maybe find myself again; I'm coming to you, to conquer the concavity of your tiny collarbone, to tear apart with my face the wet barrier of your locks while feeling the touch of our encounter every second; I bend over and take in my mouth your bra's thin, black strap, under which our only skin awaiting me loudly pounds, then with my teeth I clench the strap, pull it towards me, and glide my tongue under it, push it into your skin, and with my fingers I draw your firm body's arched opening where my gifted pendant quietly lies with a red stone that agrees so well with the paleness of your skin, then I squeeze your throat, and my hushed whispers, my I-love-yous, become barely audible, because they already reverberate inside of you, on your distant isle, where besides our deep presence, there is nothing else; we turn off the light of the room, trusting our nudity to the blemished rays reflecting through the window, whose shadows have hues that flicker over our bodies, protecting an unprotected solitude; I'm caressing your shins, squeezing your thighs, I'm sliding my fingers, they burn on your soft hips, and swim through the narrows of your groin; I melt inside of you second after second; we melt into each other second after second, the weight of my body gulps down your transparent, cotton weightlessness; the gentle movement of your fingers dug into my hair stroking the back of my neck and the arrows of your nails that every now and then pierce my skin are so pleasant; I'm titillated by the involuntary kisses of your half-dry lips on my ear and your closed eyes, which see with eyes closed, because I'm convinced that our eyes are now closed and will never open again, that from now on our bodies will live with the same rocking rhythm, and our tongues will explore each other forever, probing and discovering new worlds, and I know that you are my eternal return and I bequeath myself to you as a surprise inheritance, because, my slender girl, I have returned and have leaned my head against your shoulder. The bus is moving; the elastic reflection of a desire for a cafe blurrily appears in the glass. You wave goodbye to his wiry hair leaning against the window. The bus turns onto the intersection. The sight disappears.

It gets really cold somehow. You're shivering. Now you only dream of warm coffee or warm wine cooked over low heat with thorns plucked from thin slices of quince and peach. If you were sitting at a cafe wearing a green dress with tiny little flowers that betrayed the butterflies fluttering in your body, out of the wine and through my lips, one whole clove would suddenly plop on the tip of your tongue, because I would stretch forward, stick out my tongue and pass the clove on to your tongue, as I caress the edges of your lips. For days I thought about your only muscle that produces terror out of happiness, that appears at the speed of light and suddenly spins in my mouth with insane whirls like a flapping fish on hot ash. My heart would stop, my mouth would get dry, I would gulp down water, I would walk up to the window, and look out for a long time, following the headlights of cars passing through the street, the neon lights of shops, trying to soothe my prickling imagination. Nothing was working. Your tongue, which had cuts like exclamation marks on it, was sliding in, inside, into the depths. The soft sweet slime, almost tasting like skin, desensitized my palate with happiness and closed my eyes, and with eyes closed, I would sniff the air and then spin around the office blinded, crashing into random cabinets. I pondered for a long time, trying to comprehend the mystery of your body and character, and reaching that final conclusion that all big and crazy loves are born not from an agreement of eyes, bodies, or hearts, but from a disagreement of tongues, from their intolerant struggle until the end, and in the end their play and rhythm become apparent, their harmony and music, if they don't harm each other to the level of piercing each other like sieves, they make up before even touching each other, they're good love games, so everything is a passing succession. I'm in love with your tongue, yes, first of all just your tongue, only then you, your personality, your irises, the line of your neck, the little mole on your shoulder, your body, I don't know, your mind. I'm in love with your tongue, whose tip I'd kiss or hold with my teeth, stretch in my mouth, and shake with orgasm the next moment. And always, when I remember you, the first thing I see is your tongue-our linked and honest happiness.

And now to the cafe, the only place where you will never be alone, you will not be cold, you'll relax your muscles. What you need is filtered heat, the solitude of a cafe. You greatly rejoice when people, seeing the empty chair in front of your table, cast fascinated glances and follow the sips of your coffee. Your solitude somehow inspires familiarity and security in them, and beginning from that moment you live for the game and you play for people. You really want them to notice you, but you want them to respond in silence, see your solitude, the absent presence of your beloved girl, the so-called deep philosophical expression on your dead serious face, your sudden ahs and ohs, grrrrroans and sighs. You want people to be taken with you, completely unaware of your past, for the position you're sitting in, your facial features, and your gestures to be an opportunity for them to recreate a new life for you with new sights, new sensations, and that which did not exist, cannot exist, and will never exist, but does exist. And, in general, you thought, if people didn't exist, whose attention would you want to be worthy of? Don't know. Wait a second, I'll tell you now, one second, one second, let me tell you now, hmmm-mmmmmmmmmmmmm, okay, I would like to be worthy of the attention of birds, I would like that very much, but listen, I'm not feeling well, I'm feeling nauseous. I need to sit. You're almost there, just a few more steps, and you'll be there. Hold on, just a little more, they're waiting for you, those who know about you, but are creating you.

You leave the bus stop. You cross the street. You hit your shoulder hard against a passer-by, but there's no inclination to apologize. You walk on, looking down at the mottled asphalt. The orange hearts and light-blue rabbits pouring out of sex-shop windows flicker on your face. You walk past barbecue eateries, bra shops, baked goods and chocolate stands. Soon you turn onto a winding alley and stand in front of a colorfully painted window. It's the cafe. The beautiful shell-like green sign disperses lights at short intervals. You go in. You slowly move forward and sit at a brown wooden table. You carefully put the slumbering Bird on one of the chairs and pet its back. You hear human whispers. A few minutes later the waiter brings coffee. Warm coffee; half a spoon of sugar; the trail of steam leaving your cup melts like a sad cloud in the small space of the cafe where, besides you, two girls are sitting at a table leaning against the window. Rolling drops of water stop on the tip of your nose and separate with difficulty; they separate and plunge into your coffee with a splash. You hug the cup with both hands and hold your face over the steam. In your mind, you almost purr like Bird with half-closed eyes. The steam softly caresses your facial features, how happy I am, how happy I am, how happy, you like the cafe, there are amazing books, paintings, and photo albums here; I love you so much, you are my only close friend, let's sit for a long time, I love you so much, let's talk today until the sun sets, I have a lot to tell you; and IIII, IIII llllove yoooouuuu, vvvvery mmmmuch; I know, my love, just don't stress out, okay? beautiful girl; we'll drink coffee now; the steam caressing your lips, your nose, your lashes; the steam melts in your face, a shimmering droplet; practically untouchable it digs in, it passes without a trace, it digs in, digs in, becomes insentient, as if it were always present in its absence in some distant place, in some mysterious, non-existent shadow, for some intangible fantasy; you gulp down your coffee with the fine feathers of the steam; you imagine how the gulps thin out and tremblingly travel down like rivulets flowing through white noise, warming up your body; listen, you don't understand how beautiful your eyes are, how the colors of your irises constantly change, now that you're smiling, they turn turquoise, the tiny black sand grains in your irises melt, they almost completely disappear, at least you know, right, you know that you have amazing eyes? you, yoooooouuuuu, yoooooooourrrrssss are also vvvvery beautiful, bbbbeautiful, yes, my love, but you can't see the color of your eyes in the sun right now, if you saw it, you'd go crazy, come a little closer so the ray spreads in your irises; aaaaaaaaaaaah now they've turned completely dark blue, the color of the sea, with gentle ripples, my God, how beautiful they are, calm in the beginning, very calm, but after watching them for a long time suddenly the small ripples start to surge, no one will resist you, they have no way to resist you, yyyyyoooouuur eeeeeeyessss, tooo, they won't resist, aaaaand yooooouuuuu ddddooooon't knooooow, hoooow bbeeeaautifuul yooouuur eeeeyeeess are, they are laughing, they are laughing, they are laughing, laughing; you've put your tilted head in your hands and through the milky mist you're looking at the two girls, each with ravishing eyes, sitting at the table leaning against the window; the ray of light shines through the window and glides over the girl's sea-colored eyelashes, reaches your table and, swiping against the nose of your shoe, refracts over the floor, mmmy mmmom mmmisssses yoooouuuu, cccccooooome toooooo ooouuur hhhooouuuse ooooone daaaaayyyy; definitely, I also miss your mom very much, I remember how much we laughed; what she was explaining to us; they are laughing, they are laughing, laughing; what thin, gentle fingers, well-tended fingers, fingers that flick back the few locks that fall on your brow every now and again, that lightly ruffle your honey-colored locks after you flick back those locks; your lips slightly quiver, you smile; I see, I see for the first time your effortless smile from surprise and happiness, you're stupefied somehow, just like these two girls who are far removed from the human world, sitting at a cafe and delighting in each other, it's as if by looking they see each other eternally for the first time, they see and they delight, they see and they delight, they see and they delight, they see and they delight; with the honesty of a child, subconsciously, selflessly, thrown into the passion of delight, that bewildering ability whose homeland is childhood, to those eyes who were simply not going to break by force from those colorful balls that the clown juggled, from the soaring birds in the sky, from the red trams, which you ran after in your dreams, from the little girl with two stiff pigtails playing with a bald doll in the courtyard whom you loved like crazy and now you're convinced that you will never love anyone like that anymore; these two girls are living in a child's world, they succeeded in settling, in staying and never leaving, and they probably don't even know it; you try to remember the last time you felt simply delighted, but nothing comes to mind and suddenly, with an inner, certain voice you are convinced that it's a loss of the ability to feel delighted, that all the answers to your questions have been irrevocably erased while they were in your wet and small hand; the gentle fingers of the lock-flicking girl caress the dimple formed on your cheek, and right at that moment you feel a strange sort of familiarity, and that's why you're smiling, with the same unconscious, selfless, and honest smile, feeling a drunken happiness that bestows ringing laughter on the girls, and this is delightful; right at this moment you are delighting; you are delighting in the same way those girls are delighting and you try to hold on tightly, to fasten yourself for the surprise return of your delight; your smile widens, but your eyes start to close, your eyelids have become incredibly heavy, a deep numbness slowly conquers your consciousness, IIIII'mmmm weeeeeaaaarrring rrred nnnaaaaiiiil ppppppolish, it'sssss Frrrrrench, I'llllll gggiiiivvve yoooouuu sssome, it's nice and it'll look good on your nails, my crazy kitten, I have so much nail polish, if you want, I'll give you some, lots of it; nnnooooo, that's mmyyy Frrrench, it'sss gooood, they're laughing, they're laughing, laughing, the voices grow louder, and gradually blend into each other; you try to salvage your consciousness with one last effort, the ray of light gliding from the girl's lashes barely reaches your shoe, you somehow extend your hand, you try to make your fingers touch the ray, thinking that by touching the ray you will still be able to salvage the last little shred of your delight; they are laughing, they are laughing, laughing, laughing; and you have fallen asleep, your head on one hand, your other hand has slipped down and fallen to the ground; the smile on your face does not efface, the quivering dimple on your cheek is like evidence of your delight. Its momentary return and final goodbye.

two

I am 28 years old. That's what it says at the beginning of every page in his notebook, and he simply picks a page and writes: little boy, you have gently brought the cabbage head to the rabbit's mouth and you can feel the wavering pokes of its whiskers on your fingers; the rabbit's cheeks crunch with monotonous chomps and its whiskers release rapid lines; for you, the line's mystery is in its palpability, the line is as knowable as it is unknowable, so offer your cheek and let the rabbit's whisker-line come and prick your skin to understand your being; I know, you are veeeeeeeeeery interesting to it, feel the sweetness of its passing prickles, feel the trace on your cheek for a long time, then try to recall the sweetness of the quick and passing pain; try, even if it doesn't work, it's all the same, the line doesn't have a memory, just like the quivering feeling inside of you, the only thing that lasts is the brief moment; feel for the rabbit chomping away at the cabbage head with relish, inhaling its death, dig your fingers in the palpitating life under its soft fur, kiss its nose, and walk along the wet street; drops of rain part from the edges of roofs, and your shoulders feel their ringing weight; one drop drops right onto your nape; the chilly line glides down your spine and spreads in your blond fuzzy hairs; your fuzzy hairs are also lines–lines like flights launching into space; raindrops that spatter from your shoe noses, let them rise and fall from the edge of tiles, run into the other drops, fill up the intersecting cracks, and stream out; the drop draws its own path while your feeble feet follow it, dreaming about art;

little boy, alone in a room, in front of a mirror; fiery eyes are staring at a marvelous face; he does not feel the presence of his right hand or the surprise of his index finger pointing at the mirror; there will be many more surprises for the index finger; he sees in the mirror an unfamiliar little boy and suddenly he tries to catch the unfamiliarity of his facial features, the soft stress of his gaze, the uncatchable ripple of his hair falling down his shoulders in waves from under his beanie; your 13-year-old eyes are swollen from thoughts racing at night; you don't sleep anymore, gobbled up by beauty's thoughts; in the dim light you endlessly examine engraved patterns and feel the marks of the silver pencil under your eyes; your strength is exhausted, you need to sleep a little; you lie down, close your eyes, and see the boy in the nightshirt who gets out of bed from time to time in the dark and restlessly paces around the room with a pounding heart, not coming to terms with the agitated anxiety inside of him; outside, a cat meows, freezing your steps; the cat is a shadow and its voice is light; you pick up the silver pencil with your long fingers and press it against the paper; the line is an extension of your hand; all the flickers of the moment are passed on to the pencil through your hand: the pain of the rabbit's whisker pricking your cheek, the branched-out veins of the cabbage head, the anxiety of death, the rolling raindrops that blend with little crystals of the pencil; now your path is your hand; you draw the little boy looking at you in the mirror for the first time, and for the first time he sits in the mirror and follows how you draw yourself; he is sitting between you; all of you are alone.

You close your notebook and pick up Bird, and as you bring your mouth to its ear, you whisper that you have not seen Sahak Balayan, my friend, with little Dürer's cheeks and gentle gaze, who liked cake and playing the piano, who slept and woke up, and lived with a bow tie around his neck; I found his grave after searching for three days, I found it, yeeeeeeeaaaaaah kitttttttty, I am Schliemann; Henry Schliemann; the thirteen-year-old Dürer moved his pencil in such a way that even the author of the arm would envy him. Sahak, what you left behind was the deep tenderness of your riveted and distant gaze, which was left behind forever before you and after you in Dürer's first self-portrait, I'm afraid to look out of the window of my room, because you are always standing on a far spot of the street, a bow tie around your neck, and in your arms the rabbit you got for your birthday from one of the courtyard kids; a bow tie dying on a box in a dream, sketched with shady wings a few moments earlier and seeing the window, the clay flower pot on the window sill and the toy box, which has not been opened since the day the few-years-old coffin was put in the ground and the dust, a curtain of rough little marbles, a light-gray layer, dims memory with the silence of snow, thickening in the heart of the light each time the shutters of the window are opened, the bow tie flapping from side to side in its death throes; exhausting the strength of its wings; the unrestrained will to live; the desire to unshackle from the closed space; the lungs want to breathe; the black *mazut* fills the heart's ventricles. Every time I eat cooked chicken heart, it's like I'm eating Sahak's heart. I dig the tip of my little finger into the ventricles and pull it out. There's black bile with a sort of pleasant taste. Thick, causing giddiness. It's dissolved. Gone. The toys look more fiery in the dense darkness. But you want to dash out of the crack between the shutters, one child succeeding all the children of the world, succeeding death throes dipped in dust. If only the light-blue of your wings did not darken; your riveted gaze at the mirror. Don't be surprised, no one remembers you. I asked everyone. The old and the young of the courtyard. You did not exist. You never played piano and you never ate cake with a bow tie. When I guzzled down the strawberry-colored home-made wine at the military base, casting my eyes every now and again at the little cloud swimming in the sky and slowly smoking with regret the Montecristo No. 4 cigar given to me by Cardinal, I would think about you, feeling happy that you died young, because if you hadn't died and had come to the army, you would have committed suicide. The shoe-shining slave of the good boys every morning. For two years straight you would've cooked potatoes for them in the mess hall, you would've been their personal secretary, waiter, emptier of ashtrays, bringer and taker of news, and for your soft behind you would've been a partner in bed. The commanding officer of the company would thrash you with his feet on every occasion, he would drag you into his room and tenderize your fat body for an hour with a stick. He would force prostitution on you and you, no longer able to bear the measured strikes on your head and back, would scream out everything and tell of the every-day life of the good guys of the battalion, divulging one by one all of their financial sources. You would talk about their future plans and secret desires. Then the commanding officer of the company would spit in your face and fling you out of the room, bawling at the boys sitting around the table that you're a whore, that you told him everything, that you haven't been properly disciplined, that no one toughened you up to beatings, and from the half-cackling words slipping out of the commanding officer's mouth, your real end would begin. The boys would destroy you in the most inconceivable way for being pricked. They would prohibit you from eating in the mess hall. At night they would come to your bed and suddenly piss on your face with a generous stream or they would bring it in a glass bowl and pour it on your sheets. They would forbid everyone to shake your hand. If they saw you anywhere at the military base by yourself, they would come up to you hooting and put out burning cigarettes on your forehead or hairless arms. They would not let you take showers in the bathroom. They would steal the food sent to you from home on weekends. They would take out pictures of your mother or sister slipped in packs of cigarettes, tear them to pieces, and toss them in your face. They would force you to sit down and write to your family that you urgently need money, say, something like 100,000 drams. They would force you to pitifully describe that you have debts, because you bought necessary things on your way up to the base, say, warm socks, painkillers, valerian, lice medication, quality parts for stereos, and that if you don't pay back your debts by next week, you'll find yourself in serious trouble. You would probably stop eating food altogether. You wouldn't sleep at nights. You would anxiously wait for one of the boys' turns to visit you. A few times a day you would give yourself hope, you would take heart, comparing your life at the military base with that of guys in more grievous situations than yours, but there was no way to find a candidate who was in a more grievous situation than you, that is, not being found would simply be your unfinished desire, but you very well knew that he existed, that he, that soldier, was human; or had been human, and to shake his hand in greeting you had to be either at least God or the military base's toilet cleaner like him. Mickey Mouse. Most famous mouse. Mouse of mice. He was walking from the backyard of the mess hall through your body, with his head down, a broom in one hand instead of a gun, and in the other a big square bucket. Weightless face, round frontal bones, wide-nostril nose, sensitive mouth, seeing dreams with the sadness of a child. Your mouth was like a baby crib. Your chin was a little drawn back and you had a thin, very thin, neck. A gentle girly body or gentleness with a girly body. Your muscleless arms droop down your sturdy shoulders. The fingers stretch, streeeeeeeetch, wrapped in tight skin the color of straw, under which moving joints softly undulate like seaweed. Sometimes they would draw fingers with pencils, attempting to express the moment of movement, of stopping, of guessing the next movement, of the bonding of joint muscles, of the shadows of sockets. For anything to be cleaned at any moment, he stands ready, in your imagination, with his fingers, the broom made of twigs in one hand and the square bucket in the other. He waits with the preparedness of a Spartan soldier. You would close your eyes and ears and start to convulse like an epileptic, banging your head against the slats of the bed, but Mickey would not go away. He would not put down the bucket and broom. He would only smile softly. When your mother would visit you and ask you why you're alone, why none of your friends are with you, why you won't touch her chicken, in general why you're depressed, you don't have problems at the base, do you? You'd lose your mind and attack your mother, you'd curse her and say that she should never again try to come all the way to this distant base, and if she ever comes again, you won't even come an inch outside of the gate. I took a few deep drags of smoke and swills of wine in my mouth, and holding them in for a long time, I honestly rejoiced, because the fact of your death no longer gave you the opportunity to repeat Mickey Mouse and his mother's fate, which was always, always, without breaks and without lapses of memory, but with the same volume, it seemed, arranged in your head instead of your brain; on

Sunday, during the rotating visiting hours, all of you notice two silhouettes wandering in solitude in the farthest end of the field, which in the beginning resemble homeless dogs, but after looking for a long time it becomes clear that one of them is toilet cleaner Mickey Mouse, and the other is his redhead mother.

Not much later, you walk up to Mickey and his mother with a few guys and pop up in front of them. Good day, Auntie. Cardinal has practically entered Mickey's mother's mouth and is examining her spotty, make-up-less face. Hello. His mother gleefully replies, tightly pressing her cracked white leather purse under her arm. Auntie, Mickey Mouse is your son? Pronouncing "your" with irony, Cardinal twitches the corner of his mouth a little, which, as it turns out, is how he smiles. Her face doesn't wince. The soldiers suddenly chortle and start to uncontrollably roar with moos. Mickey's mother somehow gets confused by the unnatural laughter. She looks at Mickey, then at Cardinal, then at the soldiers, then at her son again, and then she makes an effort to smile. Pulling gently on the sleeve of his mother's dress, Mickey whispers under his breath, let's go, Mom, let's go. Where are you going? Cardinal is surprised, and with the flexible yet soft movement of his fingers he takes a thin Dutch cigar out of his breast pocket, places it between his lips, and lights it. Cardinal takes a few short puffs and blows the purple-tinged smoke in Mickey's mother's face. The woman turns away her face, trying to disperse the fog around her head with waves of her hand. We're coming with you. Cardinal continues. One of the soldiers grabs his belly with his hands and falls to the ground. Laughing and gurgling, he's screaming, aaaaaaaaah, I swear on my mother's grave, man, you're killing me, ooooooooowwww, I'm dying. He lies in the grass and rolls around, stomping his feet on the ground. Mom, come, listen, come. Mickey is already angrily pulling at his mother's sleeve. His squeaky voice reverberates from another place. Are these boys your friends? His mother asks, nervously looking at the flapping soldier on the ground. Sure, Auntie, we're Mickey Mouse's friends. We serve in the same battalion. Doesn't he write about us in his letters? He does. I'm very happy that you're my son's friends. He always writes that he's very satisfied with his service, but my son has a passport name. The woman says with a somewhat annoyed intonation. Eeeeeeh, oh Auntie, passport, passport, what passport? There's no passport. People are born again here, it's not only your son who has a new name. I'm Cardinal Gugo, this handsome guy standing next to me, my friend, kicked a crazy goal once like Zinedine Zidane, we call him Zizu for short. Every now and again we share thoughts before going to bed. I won't say this guy's nickname, you might have him arrested, because he's the base's porn film warehouse and director; he has a porn film industry. And this guy you see here, rolling on the ground like a moron, he's our Taxi, our personal taxi, whenever we want, however we want, without gas, we ride him. And the soldier standing behind me, we call him Bird, like me he's a lover of cigars, a reader of books, a strange type of bird. Oh, yeah, and he also has a secret desire to write poetry, but I doubt a new Dante will come out of Bird, just like I doubt a Gustave Flaubert will come out of me, no, bro? Cardinal turns around and winks at the smiling soldier behind him. Bird is without a hat; he has dug his hands in his pants pockets. His smile broadens at Cardinal's attention. Well, bro, recite something for auntie, let her feel your talent. Bird takes a sunflower seed out of his pocket, tosses it into his mouth and, cracking the shell and spitting it out, he takes a step forward, stands between the woman and

Cardinal, then takes on an elated and sorrowful expression on his face, raises one hand to the sky, and recites:

Nel mezzo del cammin di nostra vita
mi ritrovai per una selva oscura,
che la diritta via era smarrita.

Smaritaaaaaaaa tinnnnnnntirita, cheeee laaaaaaa dirita-aaaaaaa, that's Bird for you, eeeeeeh, poet birdie, you see, Auntie, this is how we live, who has this, eh, who? Cardinal's eyelids feebly cover the moisture of his blue irises. For a moment it looks as if all the bones in his face have become transparent under a dull pallor, as if his blood has irrevocably fermented and all his muscular fibers have withered, as if the bust of a Roman emperor is searching for a symbol in the void. Bird pulls back again. The laughter of the soldiers takes on new vigor. Roars of some unfamiliar animals fly out of Taxi's mouth who's still rolling in the grass. Mickey lets go of his mother's sleeve and waddles off. His mother has frozen and clearly fallen into the trap of Cardinal's gaze and body. Cardinal flicks half of the burning cigar between the woman's thin-stockinged legs with runs here and there, making her scream as she curls her sensitive lips: fiiiiiiiiiiiiine, enough, we're leaving! Taxi's roar instantly cuts short. He quickly gets off the ground, taps his clothes, picks up his beret, and scurries after Cardinal. Always be good friends, you only have one year left, serve without incidents, make it back to your mothers. For a moment it looks like Mickey's mother is deliriously talking to herself. But Cardinal is listening to her and without turning around he loudly yells out. But, of course, Auntie, you said it beautifully. The woman walks away slowly, catches up with her son, then they walk together, keeping a two-meter distance between each other. Moving away a little, the soldiers suddenly turn around. Cardinal takes a tomato out of his pocket, dishes out orders, passes it on to Taxi who bends over, closes one eye, and works on finding a convenient position with his body. Taxi takes a long aim at Mickey's mother's head. Pulling back his arm, he hurls the tomato with all his might. The blow seriously shakes the woman's head. The tomato explodes like a bomb from the strike. The juice of the flesh squirts out a jet of blood. The pieces and seeds scatter and fly all over. A frizzy lock of hair sticks up on Mickey's mother's head. Taxi screeches with joy at his accurate shot and starts to skip around and dance. Cardinal walks up to him, grabs his head with both hands and kisses his forehead. Mickey and his mother continue to walk without stopping, moving towards each other for a moment and then separating again, moving towards each other and separating under the ringing laughter of the soldiers, which resembles a glance suddenly cast at a little lake, scattering the serenely sleeping little fish on the surface of the turquoise water.

The bubble-popping semi-sweet strawberry-colored wine at the military base mixes with the smoke of the cigar in gulps and streams, and fills up my body. The tapered little cloud in the sky has practically disappeared. Of the little cloud, only one goose feather remains, which, stretching out, bursts into pieces and gets sucked into the blue. In that moment, dulled with joy, with a somewhat drowsy happiness, I was guessing the different ways of your suicide. My brother, you would start to attempt dying. You would axe your throat with your fingers, squeezing, then letting go; squeezing again, then letting go again. You would take a sewing pin out of the lining of your hat and lightly prick the skin of your arm. During your turn in the sniper's nest, in half an hour, you would put the barrel of the gun five times in your mouth and take it out, put it in and take it out, put it in and take it out, put it in and take it out, put it in and take it out, put it in and take it out, you would chew on the barrel of the gun. You would carve a face in sand with your index finger: eyes, a square mouth, and thin, dense furrows under the eyes. You would hit the left eye with your pinkie, as if you were pricking an iris. With a sharp-edged stone that reminded you of a prune, you would scratch slanted lines on the cheeks. Wetting your index finger you would tear two tracks down the sides of the square mouth. If you had a walnut in your pocket, a walnut that had just fallen from a long-branched tree, moist with an iodine-smelling shell, you would take it out, put it in the dark mouth, and press it until it cracked, then you would sit with the barrel of the gun leaning against your temple, you would eat the oily pieces inside the shell without shifting your gaze from the portrait's square mouth, which looked like a starless sky through foliage, or better yet, like the open door of a shed sketched in the distance around which mosquitoes revolve without touching the seductive darkness inside. And then for a moment the brown sand in the square mouth would remind you of the body of a fallen soldier, the muscles in his face wincing with pain, thumb-sized bruises on his temples with half-closed eyes, and sandy pieces of skull and brain strewn all around him. A row of white teeth would show between his lips, one leg half-bent and attached to the ground like a root, the other emphatically fixed. The nerve fibers twirled around the roots of sporadically protruding grass, with the indifference of dead earthworms, wouldn't wash themselves with the murky bucket water with blood, they would stay until they dried and burst open, softening and feeding the soil's composition. Holding the soldier by the legs, the lieutenant would drag him through the underground tunnel, but soon he would tire and stop, leaving on the layer of gravel an imprint of the trail of blood still gushing from his eye and head. He would quickly check the soldier's pockets to find a letter saying "No one is guilty," or another letter with somewhat longer contents:

"Everyone is guilty of my suicide. Is this not your creation, a mutual killing factory where time is killed until it's time to kill and where everyone is forced to wait until the next time to kill, and then the next, the next time to kill, until a sniper's bullet bores into your eye and you return home for the last time, even if it's in eternal silence in a coffin, but at home, in the living-room, where the commander of your unit sobs at the same time as your family sheds tears? And you were waiting for the war that seemed like it had started long ago, but will never end, that had ended long ago, but will never start. Me, I dreamed about the farm. I would tend cows, sheep, goats, horses, chickens, cats, bees. In the summer, I would move my bees to the mountains. I would put the beehives among the world's most beautiful and fragrant flowers, and I would live with them. At the break of dawn the sun's rays would stroke my cheek and little birds would hop and skip around my legs. I would light a small fire between two rocks and brew coffee that tasted like rays, tasted like fire, tasted like ash, tasted like flowers. I would enjoy my coffee under the buzzing of the bees and then I would go to the spring to fetch water with my chihuahua. In the middle of the day I would eat food: soft yoghurt from the village and *lavash*[4] baked in a *tonir*;[5] I would eat slowly,

---

4 Type of flat bread typically baked in a *tonir*, or underground oven.

5 A type of underground oven used for baking or roasting.

very slowly; at first I would dig my spoon in the yoghurt and take it to my mouth, then I would bite off a piece of *lavash*, I would take some yoghurt again, I would look at the flowers, at their swaying heads in the wind and at the track opened up in the grass. My chihuahua, joyously shaking his head and body, would be occupied with bones and stew, then I would sprawl in the grass and read Saroyan or Chinese fables in that favorite pocket book of mine, in which there were fabulous names like Xiu Na, Tsi Yoy, Xiu Shi, Tszi Tszi Tszo, or Tszo Tszo Tszi, Oh My. But it's already too late, you did nothing for me to have a farm, to keep bees, and go fetch water with my chihuahua; even though you haven't even done anything, it's just that I shuffled everyday into this slaughterhouse, I saw you, I hung out with you, I talked to you, because all armies are slaughter-houses that are governed by elders, all commanders, all armed soldiers, all leaders who call to arms and fire, and for history build their heroic deeds with the taste of flesh and blood, and for what? For nothing. Simply for regular murders and conquests of rich areas. Armed with guns, grenades, and bullets: an army prepared to cut throats; regular minced meat; with an inner world based on a lie, without an army, the slaughterhouse will calm down, without soldiers, the voices will disappear, the barracks will cave in, and in their place lush grass will grow and ripple in the cleansing wind. It's up to you to see whether you understand what a chihuahua is, what a bee is, who Tszi Tszi Tszo is; eh, in short, seriously there's no desire to spend two years with animals like you. Even when I'm discharged, you'll be with me for the rest of my life, but I want to forget you, and this is why I'm shooting straight into my mouth so that you completely vanish together with my splattered brain. I'm saying that you're all guilty, that I'm dying, that it happened, but not because I'm committing suicide, but because

I'm dying without having kept bees, without having had a chihuahua, without having drunk coffee while watching the heads of flowers.

Fuck all of you and everything that's good to you, BYYYYYYEEEEEEE!"

Or another letter:

"This can't go on: beatings every day, humiliation, the guys don't respect me, I have no friends, no one even greets me anymore. I'm all alone. The commanding officer of the company cursed me in every way possible, I was too scared to say anything, I've lost my self-love, my senses have completely dulled. The guys throw table-cleaning cloths at my face, they make fun of me at every occasion, they throw oily table-cleaning cloths at my back. When they throw them in my face, I don't care that much, but when they throw them at my back, I take it very badly. I want to fight and I do fight, but neither for life, nor death. I fight for what I don't remember; I fight for the moment before my birth, for taking a step forward and detaching myself from life and death. I'm calm somehow; I'm completely calm, because no one knew that I was going to be born and no one would remember that I was born. No one remembers the soldiers who died in the Trojan War, what they felt, how they lived, what they dreamed about, but I feel closer to them than all the Achilleses and Odysseuses. Don't give this letter to my father."

Or:

"Almost every day the lieutenant humiliates me and tortures me with beatings, I don't even know why anymore, he doesn't know either, it's become automatic, from force of habit, every day at the same hour he comes in drunk and latches onto me, he asks about the rights and obligations of squad commanders, but without getting a chance to reply, he beats me, hitting my back and sides with the butt of his gun, then cursing me, he waits until I can't resist not answering, not defending myself, so that he can continue beating me. When I called home asking you for money, it was the lieutenant who forced me, telling me that he needed to buy a gift for his girlfriend's birthday, that he had important costs to pay off, that he has to buy medicine for his father who's in ill-health. The lieutenant lives in a village next to the base, and every day after the evening formation, he forces me to go down to his house, to cook dinner for them, to turn on the heater, and heat bath water. During the last rotation, he didn't let any one of us in the unit sleep for five days, take off our shoes, or wash ourselves, because one of the boys had apparently not been able to properly report back on the rotation, and he was looking for every opportunity to come up with new punishments. They say that he's related to one of the generals and that he won't even yield to the commander. Yesterday he came and dragged me away, beat me, I fell to the ground, he beat me for an hour, he wouldn't even let me at least cover my face with my hands, he was cutting up the skin of my fingers with a knife, he was stabbing my legs, he was saying, look straight into my eyes, then he tore off my pants, he pulled down his pants and underwear, he wanted to, but it wasn't working, I was thrashing around like a lunatic, I had closed my eyes, I was praying to myself to not pass out, I clenched my jaws with all my strength, there was no way he could open my mouth, in the end he kicked me in the forehead with his knee, he crouched down and set fire to my eyelids, my eyebrows, the skin of my face here and there, he pulled up his pants and left, promising that next time he would do it and tell the guys if I don't agree to it willingly. I don't want to live anymore, I can't somehow, it's not working for me. I held my automatic to his head a few times at night when he was asleep; I wanted to shoot, I couldn't do it, my hands were shaking, but I really wanted to, if I didn't feel scared, I would definitely shut him up, but one day one of the soldiers of the company, someone stronger than me, will surely do it. Guys, I want you to know that I'm not a whore. My writing is not whorish. Believe me, please, the lieutenant did not get what he wanted, he couldn't get it, I didn't let him. Please, don't curse me behind my back, just know that one day you'll find yourself in my situation. Bury me next to grandpa. I'm sorry, Mom."

The lieutenant would quickly burn all the half-frayed letters with all those words with a lighter, and then he would squash the ash into the gravel with his heel, he would light a cigarette and wait for the arrival of the commanders and police at the base. The green, circular patterns on the outfit of the dead soldier would resemble reedless marshes, and the potato-colored ones would resemble waterholes. I wonder if there are fish in the marshes? Next week you could have taken a hook, come, sat for hours on the hot peat and watched the swaying reeds and the rippling moss under the water. But suddenly you would hunt for yourself, walking barefoot through the waterholes, you would walk up to the soldier's mouth, crouch down, take a cigarette out of the pack, put it between his lips, and light it. Smoke, my brother. Until they come and get you, as long as no one's around, smoke as much as you want. Who knows when you'll have free time again? I'll stand in for you. He smokes, without hurrying, his face relaxes. You take his smoking body, throw it over your shoulder and vigilantly stand next to the gun on the ground. You would smudge that portrait with three of your fingers and pace up and down again. You would freeze in your tracks and suddenly put the barrel of the gun in your mouth. This time you would put your finger on the trigger. It would seem slippery. Your finger would loosen. The barrel would slip down your mouth. As you shaved in the morning, you would suddenly press the razor against your throat and you would close your eyes in the mirror. The skin-coated razor would press against your throat, but it would bound back like a spring. When there was no one in the barracks in the morning, you would go in, walk up to your mesh base bed, take off your belt, tie one end to a slat, and, lying down on the floor, you would throw the noose around your neck, and then you would slowly succumb to your body's weight. Which method would you choose? In those days nothing was of any interest to your mind anymore but choosing a method of suicide, all of your thoughts and reasons were aimed at a method for reaching the final deed. Searching for ideas in all of this and fighting for all of this would be a pointless waste of time and effort for you, because you can't search for what has already been found. You can't fight for what is already given. What would stay behind is the inexhaustible method that made for the exceptional moment to feel the unrepeatable singularity of your life, to feel the last minutes of your life. What notes would you take? Which rendition would play in your head? The music would probably give you courage. And upon suddenly finding the method of death, reality would be felt for the first and last time.

The wine and smoke seem to have numbed your body. Your head is spinning. You walk to the underground bunker and go in. It seems as if you're sitting in the aroma of chicken soup. You eat slowly, constantly stirring your spoon in the bowl. You leave the buckwheat and chicken wing to the end. Before the rotation, you need to sleep well, to rest your brain, to let go of every bit of leftover stress. The enemy likes surprises. But you never fall asleep during rotation. You're a good service man. You even received a decoration with a bear paw. You build a pyramid with your spoon, flatten the top, push the chicken wing into it, then demolish it by eating the buckwheat from the bottom, and in the end you carefully nibble on the wing, suck on the bones, and make a pile on the outer edge of your plate. You go to the bathroom with the spoon in your hand. You take the box of washing powder out of the gray cabinet in the corner. You pour powder from the torn corner of the box into your spoon, put it in your mouth, and swallow. Your palate and esophagus burn from the soft bitterness. It's as if all of the blood in your body collects in your chest and stands face-to-face with a huge artificial dam. You go back to the bunker. If Door had a mind, it would party today. You say that to yourself, lying down and covering your body with hope. Door is the base dog, a mix of shepherd and chihuahua. Her head is the size of an apple and her muzzle is pressed inward. Her eyes are always red with fatigue, rolling restlessly. Her body is big, her butt is hanging, and half of her tail is docked. Her tongue flows out of her fangs like a streamlet. Her coat looks like it's covered in mud. Every few months you eat Door's pups, when they open their little eyes and look at the sun. A feeling of joy at the acquaintance with the pear-shaped fiery droplet makes their fur tingle, and the fathomless space of the sky sets their curly tails in motion. Door is suckling her pups in a boat-like hollow, then she runs out to bark, turns around again, suckles, and runs out to bark. A few times, apprehending the diversionary attacks of the enemy and belligerently raising the alarm, Door saved the base and the lives of the group. I've seen how raindrops settled on the coats of Door's pups; I've seen it and held my breath. Suddenly the space is disrupted by reflective flickers, the eye hunts for fallen freedom, and space begins to slowly flow and sound becomes audible. The raindrops settle on the coats of the pups and freeze without trembling, but with weightless tenderness. If I were God and I looked down at the boat-like hollow, it would seem to me as if I were looking at a delightful flower with pink petals, on the surface of which, in the frozen little rain crystals, my entire creation would be reflected. But I'm not God. Every day, before falling asleep I get surprised and annoyed. For instance, how terrible it would be if I were God. I would give humanity psychological peace, yeah, that's all, psychological peace and the gift of surprise every moment, so that when people, animals, and plants meet each other they get amazed and call out "OH MY," but now, every night, until I fall asleep, I have to get annoyed and think about why I'm not God and why I shouldn't be able to see and enjoy the beauty of a flower. In the beginning we ate Door's pups to blow our own horns and to be a little weird, and then it just became a habit. We fried their little hearts with onions and bell peppers, and before putting them in our mouths, we would display them under the candlelight tweezed between our index fingers and thumbs and examine them for a long time. Every few months Door gives birth in the same deathly hollow and waits for its emptying. When one of us slaughters the pups, Black, one of the good guys at the base, covers his ears with both hands and screams aaaaaaaaaaaaaaaaaaaaaaaaaaaaaaaaaaaaaaaaaaaaaaaaaahhhhh-hhhhhhhhhhhhhhhhhhhhhhhhhhhhhhhh; Black screams aaaaa aaaaaaaaaaaaaaaaaaaaaaaaaaaaaaaaaaaaaaaaaaaaaaaaaaaaa aaaaaaaaaaaaaaaaaaaaaaaaaaaaaaaaaaaaaaaaaaaaaaaaaaaaa aaaaaaaaaaaaaaaaaaaaaaaaaaaaaaaaaaaaaaaaaaaaaaaaaaaah-hhhhhhhhhhhhhhhhhhhhhhhhhhhhhhhhhhhhhhhhhhhhhhhhhhh-

hhhhhhhhhhhhhhhhhhhhhhhhhhhhhhhhhhhhhhhhhhhhhhhhh-
hhhhhhhhhhhhhhhhhhhhhhhhh and flees into the forest. We
bark after him woof woof woof woof woof woof woof woof
woof woof woof woof, oooooooooooooooooooowwwwww-
wwwww, Black can no longer hear. He's entered the depths
of the forest and is grazing grass. Every now and again Black
grazes fresh grass like a sheep and suddenly screams innocently
aaaaaaaaaaaaaaaaaaaaaaaaaaaaaahhhhhhhhhhhhhhhhhhhh-
hhhhhhhhhhhhhhhhhhh. Door does not leave the side of the
slaughtering soldier, she only tilts her head a little and attentively watches to the end, twitching her eyes every now and
again. After the hollow has been emptied, she approaches and
licks the soldier's bloody fingers. Door never eats the bones of
her pups. In general, ever since we started to eat her pups, Door
has become vegetarian. She stays away from meat and bones,
she prefers porridge, bran, stone, bark, mushroom, root, absolutely anything but meat. I've seen Door carry the bones and
heads of her pups one by one with her teeth a little away from
the base, bury them in the ground, then return to the empty
hollow, sniffling it and lying in it. Milk flows out of Door's teats,
filling the hollow. This is the only time Door is silent. In the
morning she wakes up, steeped in her own snow-white milk.

You park Cardinal's blood-colored Mustang in front of the
cemetery gate, in the melon-looking shade hanging from the
gate. As she extends the keys of the Mustang parked in front of
"Dear Done" strip club on Teryan Street, Nona softly chuckles
and says that she hasn't changed the CD in the car stereo, which
was the CD that Cardinal had listened to for the last time on
the day he went to the army. The fiery dancer's outfit that Nona
is wearing looks torn; her body and outfit clash. She's tall, restless, and happy. In the beautiful stereo with sparkling lights is

Pink Floyd's album *The Final Cut.* On the road you think that Cardinal probably drank on that day and listened mostly to "The Gunner's Dream" as he drove around the city. You turn on the stereo and press track 5. The melody saturates the car. In the car you suddenly sense the gentle, frightening scent of Cardinal's cologne. The car moves forward with the persistence of a hard drop of blood, moving from street to street, and crossing intersections, slowing down like a sharp, unstoppable knife.

Parked by the cemetery gate in the melon-looking shade, you listen to the song one more time, casting a glance every now and again out of the side window at the dog sleeping in a ray of sun not far from the car with a butterfly swarming around it. You get out and close the car doors. Following his uncle's directions, walking past broken cross-stones and through sporadically fenced-off spruces, trampling old headstones almost completely buried into the ground, you find Sahak's grave. The location of his buried body still exists, it hasn't been thrown out yet and will resist for another half a century. No one has visited it in a while. Between the sun-scorched shrubs and thorny bushes, the red tufa gravestone with thick curved lines of big and small tracks of urine comes into view. Tipped against the stone is a sooty, yellow-streaked cup with ruffled brims for burning incense that looks like the helmet of a soldier killed in war many years ago. A grasshopper skips over the peaks of tall, wave-like stringy grass and stops at the edge. You lightly kick the cup with the tip of your shoe. The grasshopper is unresponsive, as if it were in deep, dead numbness. You stand over Sahak for a long time. You light a cigar. This time there wasn't enough money for the Count. You bought a "Willem II." Cardinal liked this thin, veiny, mild Dutch cigar. The ray of sun pleasantly warms your neck without burning it.

You smoke slowly. You stroke the sensitive veins of the Dutchman with your finger. You're standing in such a way that your soles, which oppress the ground, do not somehow harm the fingers of your friend's skeletonized body. When you finish the cigar, you flick away the butt. You walk up to the gravestone. You lick your finger and draw a space on the surface of the stone with super straight borders, giving your friend a new room to make himself comfortable and play the piano. Then you see yourself in a dream lying on a tiled floor drinking tea with your feet sunk into the gut of a slaughtered sheep. When you swallow, you suddenly feel a strange flutter on the surface of your lips. You pull away abruptly. You carefully look into the cup. It's Sahak's eyes. You nervously sink your fingers into the cup. You grab the slippery eyes and take them out. You throw them on the floor. After a while, the flapping ends. You take the spoon and put the eyeballs on the brim of the cup, and then you blow up the membranes with the handle. Sticky mazut pours out like lava and fills into the tea. You drink and wait. It's as if your throat is being scraped with the hot tip of a knife. You feel sharp pangs in your lungs. You're gasping for air. You try to scream. Your mouth won't open. The mazut has dried and glued your lips together. Your eyes detach from their sockets and fall on the tiled floor. The drops of black liquid burst in the air with pops. You jump up. There's an indifferent silence in the bunker. The light of the candle is blowing shadows. You bury your head under the pillow; Sahak is coming after you, see, he doesn't have a tongue, but he's coming; do you remember him? I remember him; I'll tell you about it now;

The smell of a sewing machine always emanated from Sahak. Every day in the summer, his piano's rough and crude chords trickled out of the window of the first-floor apartment from the third entrance of our building. His birthday was the first time in my life that I received a special invitation on a card. My mother had prepared a gift for him. It was a box wrapped in green cardboard. Years later when I asked my mother what was in the box, she said it had been a little deer antler comb. With the gift pressed tightly under my arm and after several failed attempts, I managed with a quick jump to push the bell of their apartment door. His mother opened the door. Sahak was leaning against her long leg. He welcomed me with a sad look in his eyes and a wrinkled black suit. Around the collar of his white shirt, he had tied a bow tie whose crooked tip every now and then brushed against the rolls of his chin. He was holding a leather-bound trunk decorated with the heads of long-haired Native Americans, and he made it clear, by jiggling his cheeks, that the presents should be put in it. One by one, we walked up to him, congratulated him, and put our gift in the trunk. When the turn came to one of the children who was holding a white rabbit, Sahak took a few steps back and froze. With the same expression on his face, he now looked at the rabbit, now at the trunk, now at the rabbit, now at the trunk. He was licking the corner of his mouth with the tip of his tongue. The rabbit was nibbling on a small bite of cabbage, its whiskers were twitching, and its ears flapping. Sahak put the lid on the trunk and moved up to him with tiny steps, carefully picked up the animal with both hands, then brought his cheek up to its whiskers and gently pressed it against them. A smile of happiness shone on his face. Sahak never put the rabbit down again. From that moment on no one paid attention to him anymore. We were playing hide-and-seek, soldier-soldier, we were jostling each other and eating fruit, while Sahak, in turn, was indifferent to all of us, occupied with a watermelon. He would greedily fill his cheeks with the meat of the fruit, lightly exert force on his jaws to first squeeze, then swallow the pieces without chewing for a long time, not once raising his head to the children sitting at the table. Then, when it was time for the cake, he blew out the candles and, impatient for his mother to cut it up, attacked it and started to eat it with relish. He digs his finger in the cream, licks it, rubs it on his tongue, then squishes the ripped pieces of cake and shoves them in his mouth, and in the end wipes his creamy fingers on his back. Sahak probably thought that his eating would make him forget our presence, but we were not in a hurry to leave. When he got up completely bloated and walked up to the Petrov piano, we got that we had to scatter as fast as possible, but it was impossible, the sad look on his mother's face pleaded with us to stay and listen to her son's rendition. Forced, we unhappily approached the piano and perched around it. Sahak carefully placed the rabbit on top of the piano, plopped on the moving chair, hung his head over the keys, and started. In the beginning, he played insecurely and a little scared. He constantly stuck his tongue in and out and wet his lips, which probably still had the sweetness of the cake. He now looked at the rabbit on top of the piano, now at his own fingers, now at the rabbit, now at his fingers, but soon, rediscovering his courage, he suddenly ran after the sense of the melody. I was amazed at his meaty, slow-moving fingers that had become supple and stretched, harmonizing with the keyboard and the demand of the perfect rendition of the piece. He was playing without notes. His drool streamed from the edge of his lips. His mouth no longer closed and his big head sunk into his massive shoulders more and more. In the end, only the playful elastic movements of his fingers were visible which filled the room with delightful music. Sahak struck the last chord and spasmodically shook his head, stretching his fingers pointedly in the air like arrows that looked taller than him. An applause exploded. One of the kids took a carnation out of the vase on the table and ceremoniously presented it to Sahak, chuckling under his breath. Refusing the flower, he turned around, took the rabbit off the piano, hugged it, and walked up to the festive table again. Choosing a ruffled piece from the already-smashed cake, he started to eat it, not forgetting in the beginning to carefully lick the cream.

Three months later, he was playing in a half-dilapidated factory and he fell into a mazut reservoir and drowned. We saw him a lot around the abandoned factory. It's as if he noticed us. He would approach us, stand next to us, and not say a word. Wherever we went, Sahak would follow us, stand next to us, and not say a word. We would beat him anxiously, threaten to crush his head with stones if he didn't stop following us. It's as if he noticed us. Sahak would come after us, stand next to us, and not say a word. When we climbed trees and ate mulberries for hours, he would come, stand under the tree, extend his hand, and not say a word. When we played football and struck the ball next to the goal, Sahak would suddenly appear with a bow tie tied to his neck, a muddy shirt, and the ball in his hands. He would hand over the ball to us, stand next to us, and not say a word. I wondered about him and asked myself, could it be that as he was drowning he waited for one of the kids to see him by chance and save him? When the heavy black mazut was pouring into his lungs, did he understand that he would no longer be? How did he understand his not being? Does being differ from not being? Was one of his last wishes in the trunk full of toys? Had he spoken, could he have been saved? Had we been quiet, could he have been saved? Had he noticed us that day and followed us, could he have been saved? I tried very hard to recall even one word that came out of his mouth.

There's silence. Sahak had been lain in a brown polished coffin in the same suit he wore on his birthday. The bow tie was stuck sadly to his neck. His meaty fingers were resting on his chest. The coffin suited him a lot.

The Mustang is parked in the same place, in the same unchanging position. The dog is still sleeping and the butterfly is restless. The butterfly probably thinks the dog's dead. You walk up to it to be sure. It looks like there's a square heart beating in the dog's abdomen that's trying to burst out with a powerful quake every now and again. The dog is sleeping, because it's breathing. The butterfly stubbornly won't leave, probably thinking it's dead. You sit in Cardinal's car and turn on the engine. He had been given the Mustang on lease and had entrusted it to his lover Nona, the dancer at "Dear Done" strip club on Teryan Street, two years before going to the army. Talking about the car made her squint and made spots the color of the Mustang appear on her cheeks, but her emotions were instantly veiled by anger devised on the spot with some sort of feigned fit. You turn on the engine of the small horse and press the play button on the stereo. His heart beats with a gurgle, but he is a robust and immortal youth. Cardinal is buried at the other end of the city, but you have decided that if you find Nona, you'll say that you were friends with him, and you would ask her to lend Cardinal's car for a few hours and you would get her approval; if that happened, you would not visit him, instead you would drive the car, because Cardinal said that the Mustang was his home, his bread and water, his everything, that he very often spent the night in the car, and that he never had it washed, but that he washed it himself with special expensive polishing liquids. If the Mustang is his home, then it's his coffin and grave, you think. The splendid red leather squeaks restlessly under your movements. You press the button on the stereo, put on the song "One of the Few," and turn up the volume. The clock is ticking. Cardinal's splendid coffin slowly turns, goes down the broad street, and moves towards the city.

Make them mad, make them sad, make them add two and two. Make them me, make them you, make them do what you want them to. Make them laugh, make them cry, make them lie down and die.

I was lying in the hospital with pneumonia. I had just, just started to walk. In the beginning they brought the food to my room, but when I got a little better, they told me I had to get the food myself. The little mess hall was at the very end of the hallway, and in order for there to be food left for me and for me to make it in time, I was forced to leave twenty minutes earlier, leaning against the cold wall, barely scraping forward, and resting on seats on the way. That day, when I entered the mess hall, the table had already been set, the half-transparent steam was rising from soups in pots, and the tableware had been arranged with care. I noticed that the soldiers standing by the tables were somewhat restlessly waiting and not sitting in their chairs. My head was spinning, I somehow fell into my chair, the soldier standing next to me tapped my shoulder with his hand, bent over, and whispered in my ear, get up, Cardinal is coming, if he sees you sitting, it won't be good. Who's Cardinal, I asked. What do you mean, you don't know? It's Cardinal Gugo, he's the one who watches the battalion and hospital, get up, I tell you! A thousand and one legends were told about Gugo. They said he had a seriously evil character and that he never forgave a misstep, they said he had bitten off the unit commander's finger, they said he had an awesome room and

that beautiful girls came to him. They said Gugo was supposedly an adopted child and when he found out about it he drank
for twenty days without sleeping, they said he only smoked
cigars and listened to opera and rock and beat the soldiers
into listening with him. They said it was impossible to resist
Cardinal Gugo's gaze, that he was not physically strong, but that
he beat up anyone. In short, my impressions of Cardinal were
legendary, and now I had the chance to be a participant in yet
another legend. I didn't move out of my seat and I scornfully
looked at the soldier's face holding his stomach. Suddenly a
deep silence reigned. Thin as a thread on a spindle, a tall, very
tall guy walked through the door. It was Cardinal. There was
a book pressed under his arm. He was wearing a white fuzzy
robe, a white shirt under it, and white pants. Cardinal Gugo
was white, and there was only one part of him that clouded
that whiteness: his pale and sad face. That face looked like it
was trying, every second, to cover up an invisible pain that
rolled through his body and soul. I later thought a lot that a
guy with a face like that cannot be that evil, that more likely it
was a sort of deceptive evil that he had required for his own life.
He probably genuinely thought that this was the only way he
could live at the base and in life in general. Cardinal walked up
to me with gentle steps, stopped at the head of my table, fixed
his gaze in my direction, measured me from head to toe, and
let out a TSK. Everyone quietly sat down. The soldier poured
soup from the pot in his plate. HMM, Cardinal continued and
started to slowly eat. The soldiers took a breath and fell on the
food. In the course of this, I paid attention to the way Cardinal
was holding his spoon, embracing the handle with his index
finger and thumb almost untouchably, but most striking was
his raised pinky, which gently swam with the movement of his
hand. It seemed to me that this raised pinky was the center of

his life and the essence of his noble spirit. After the mess hall they told me that Gugo was calling me to the garden. It was autumn. Cardinal was sitting under a tree, reading a book on a bench. From a distance it looked like a magic white bird had descended on the yellowed garden. I somehow approached him and greeted him. He closed the book and I read the cover: Gustave Flaubert, *Madame Bovary*. Do you know who I am? No, I answered. Do you see this knife? Gugo continued and from between the pages he took out a wide blade knife. Yeah. I'm going to stab your heart with it. If you're going to stab, stab. Cardinal raised his head and looked straight into my eyes. It was hard to withstand his gaze, but I somehow withstood it and turned away my face. Your friends called for you. I know, I said indifferently and turned my gaze to the book. So you're reading *Madame Bovary*? Cardinal's pale face immediately radiated at the pleasant surprise. It's my thirty-seventh time, brother. I also like *Madame Bovary*, I've read it. And it started. I've never met anyone in my life yet who liked Flaubert's novel that much. Cardinal immediately made sure that I was moved to his room. We were living like we were in the 19th century, wearing long robes, strolling around our room, smoking cigars, sipping on cognac, and Gugo reading from *Madame Bovary*, rejoicing at random sentences. Bless my Emma. If I ever have a daughter, my friend, I've decided to call her Emma, the first time I read it, I was knocked senseless. The second she committed suicide, I cursed that Flaubert so much my tongue burned. Cardinal would read all night, then he would hand the book over to me and ask me to read my favorite passages, but I got scared in a way that he would be disappointed by my choices. He almost knew the entire book page by page, he even knew what Emma was wearing in what passage. If only I could take Leon's place, eh, at least once! Cardinal told me that he had not read any other book in his life and that he doesn't want to read any other book, that the book always pulls him in more and more each time he reads it. Cardinal Gugo and Emma Bovary were like each other, both were melancholic and exceedingly fascinating. When Gugo felt better, he would start to cry and describe Emma's funeral, then, as always, he would remember Flaubert's father, mother, and wife. I would say that to my knowledge Flaubert didn't have a wife, only lovers. And that's why he killed Emma, if he had had a wife and loved her, he wouldn't have touched her, Gugo would scream. I somehow resisted laughing, putting a dramatic expression on my face. Cardinal and Madame Bovary met each other a century and a half later, and that meeting was inevitable. I was in a deep sleep one night when my friend woke me up and invited me to sit at a table set between the beds in the dark. I sleepily asked. What happened? I heard a hoarse voice. Cardinal was killed an hour ago, they said that he'd already been discharged, that his military booklet had been in his pocket, that he had been stabbed about twelve times with a knife. The boys want to drink, are you coming? I sat on my bed and leaned against the cold wall. No, have fun, I don't feel well, thanks, I want to sleep. I didn't want to drink to Cardinal, I dreamed of getting discharged and reading *Madame Bovary* again.

The city swirls in the whirlpool of the shiny silver rims of the Mustang, the lampshades of its streets, the trees, the pharmacies, the signs of sex shops and banks, the beauty salons, chocolateries and teahouses, the citrus fruit booths covered in posters, the real estate agencies, the windows of bookstores and pizzerias, the delight in the gaze of bald cream-colored mannequins looking at the street out of shoe stores and fashion boutiques; a cat perched on the brims of garbage cans with broken lids, a woman with a pom-pom hat, a yellow box pressed under her arm, people who are walking, every now and again casting their glance at the flowerpots on the balustrades of gondola-shaped balconies of buildings, the green stems hanging from the edges of the flowerpots are happy in their drooping state, the space of the sky interrupted by clouds, the beak of a crow falling like a stone from the top of a poplar, the petrified exclamations of parking lot attendants with orange shirts and black faces scorched by the sun, the whispers of conversations in a café and the writing in pen in the notebook of an apron-wearing waiter, or, more precisely, the thick, flowing ink of the pen and the nice scent of the ink, just like that of soap which you constantly want to bite and eat, but don't bite and don't eat; roasted chestnut shells that naughty sparrows steal, steal and throw on sidewalks, throw and steal in the middle of streets, the scattered newsstands and right next to the news-papers tobacco, lighters, news, prepaid phone cards, lottery tickets, not far in the back, fruity cigarettes lined up with care on crossword puzzles, branches fallen from trees with mostly dry, dead bark, on the same street, with the same bearing, it seems like they are trying to live again, because they have been relegated to indifference, just like the dog in the middle of the broad Saralanj road that was mangled under the wheels of a car, the color of asphalt, it's been two weeks that it's been lying on the road, as if it should be this way, one of the dog's legs is disobediently raised, or, more precisely, its tendon, skinless, thin as a scraped sour *lavash*; the dog died with a tendon up in the air, and the branches of the tree that fell in the street look impregnated with new roots, but those are unfinished dreams; a snake has opened its mouth on the pediment of a pharmacy, hanging its terrifying crooked tooth on your neck, the snake has a narrow eye, split with a razor; old wooden windows with cracked glass, attached flakes of paint, a network of thick, rat-colored cobwebs in the openings; somewhere around here you were born and slurped on ice cream, drank cold *kvass* with crumbs of bread, tasted round sugary cotton candy, played with an empty bottle of *Jermuk* and took off your shoe when you kicked the *Jermuk* bottle at the goal; the voices of the boys in the neighboring courtyard can no longer be heard, they've all scattered around the world to find work or they died, one or two of them stayed addicted to drugs, the rest got sentenced for theft, the boys: confident, arrogant, they dressed like real princes and kept Great Danes like English lords; now there are no more Great Danes either, because the lords left, abandoning time and the city; the banana peel leaves its imprint on the tile, just like thousands of years ago an ancient mosquito gave up its life on the surface of a rock; the red dragon at the tattoo parlor dancing in the stars, it's probably still a baby, its wavering saw-like tail brushes against the wing of a star; the sorrel soup at the "Tavern," the yellow-streaked sorrel seeds or the *tan*6 of the soup, the cleansing feeling of your mind chases a whole new rapture of lonely happiness in your soul; a multitude of people flushes out of Yeritarsadakan7 like muddy waters, why are they always dressed in black, those seals dragging their bodies over beach rocks, hurling exclamations along the street, maybe they see black dreams and wash themselves with black water in the morning; the defined muscles of football players and the tousled hair of the boys a moment before kicking the ball, the kits of Barça and Chelsey posted on the walls of Vivaro and Toto bookmakers; there are no bakeries anymore, and until the

---

6   *Tan* is a type of cold drink made of yoghurt mixed with water.

7   Yeritasardakan is a metro station in Yerevan.

intersection stretched in rows and in between the rows are little boys in warm coats tightly holding on to bread coupons; the coupons would get wet, they would get holes in them, because it was the sensation, the sensation of the little boys to bring home bread that made the palms of their hands sweat, but there are still bread ovens; when you walk at night you look at the shadows of your wiry uncombable hair on the tufa of buildings; the air wafts out of the window and brings with it the scent of freshly baked bread, roasted crust, and the rising of kneaded dough; you stop; you turn around, enter the bakery, and buy warm, skin-scorching bread from kind-hearted women with floury arms wearing white gowns, and you eat it on the way saying oh-oh, rapidly chewing, because your palate is burning or, more precisely, you nibble like a rabbit on the edges, the red hot bites of the crusts, and your heart relaxes; now the courtyard *gampr*8 no longer exists; you curled up against its heaving belly in front of the entrance of your building, on the first floor, so that you wouldn't die of cold in the freezing weather, because you had eaten the long-awaited bread on your way home and you were afraid to go in empty-handed; and here, gathered around nightclubs is a group of fiery-dyed young hair and wrinkled masks, some of them drinking beer, making jokes and dancing, writhing their supple bodies; in the windows of gay clubs and ordinary houses, green movements flicker, maybe it's the name of the curtains and ordinary houses, "Virgin Dream," "Between My Legs, In My Soul," "75 Sheets," in some place or other they are mourning a young man who died of pneumonia, they are disgusted with life and

---

8   The Armenian Gampr is a dog breed typical to the Armenian Highlands, similar in some ways to the Caucasian Shepherd.

are tying a black ribbon with gold letters so that everyone can see his age and they can rock their grieving heads, the doors of a trolleybus open and close with dry creaks; the sharpness of the shawarma-cutting knife makes you laugh, the uprooted molars on the heads of entrances of dental clinics are covered with a hardened layer of gray dust, you're short, you won't reach the molar, whenever you walk past one you want to leave a trace with your finger in the gray film on the molar; the endless pomegranates in souvenir shops are nerve-wracking, the golden, obsidian, wooden crosses with Jesus and without Jesus, and pomegranates, pomegranates, pomegranates, pomegranate ashtrays, pomegranate pendants, pomegranate candlesticks, pomegranate who knows motherfucking what, motherfucking cross; sssssssssssssssssss, vomit would spill into the sieve from indelicacy and misery, while the idea of scarecrows on souvenir crosses, which are not bad, have now become pieces of mud from repulsion; animal appetite for pomegranates and crosses, as if to say we're old creators, we still feel the moist of civilization, we are as old as God or Rome, old sheep; you're very tempted to throw a stone to shatter the window and the gazes of those hideous, talentless, insipid pomegranates and crosses; through the little window of *Berliner Wurst*, you look at the grainy cinnamon-colored smears of the sauce that paint the sausage, the sauce is hot, very hot, slowly cooking your tongue and throat with fire, thank you, please come again, the sausage is yours, you smile, because what awaits you are the white stairs of the Cascade and the enjoyment of the tasty and hot sausage in front of the city's panorama in the wind's pleasant drafts; little drops of sap have frozen on the leaves of trees, the flowers are not tended well: they're bothered and closed; the rhythms of the city–its ephemeral movements–refracting in the rims of the coffin and disappearing with sparks into the water-colored air.

A few cars coming in the opposite direction give happy signals, probably because they recognize Cardinal's Mustang. You don't reply to the signals. You park the car in front of a shop, you go in and buy a beer; you wink at the saleswoman when you pay and you walk out to get in the car; you turn around again; you approach the saleswoman, wink at her, and she smiles; you smile. Before driving the car, you open the bottle, turn on the engine, and take off. You put the bottle to your mouth as you drive and drink it in two-three gulps; you drive and drink. Cheers to you, my friend. It's time to take the Mustang back to Nona. From your coat pocket, you take out a few crumpled pages that you tore out of Flaubert's *Madame Bovary*, and among those pages are some of Cardinal's favorite passages, then you open the glove compartment of the coffin and put the papers in the deepest, darkest corner. Nona is standing by the entrance of the strip club restlessly pacing back and forth. You park the car in the same place, in the same position. You get out swinging the bottle in your hand and smiling at Sona. She quickly takes the keys, complains about her sleeplessness, then she kisses your cheek, says goodbye, and hurriedly enters the club. The trace of Nona's lipstick titillates as you walk. As you cross the intersection, Door suddenly pops up in front of you, dragging its pink tongue over the ground. You put the bottle on the sidewalk, get up on Door's tongue, and sit on the soft couch that reminds you of a split walnut shell. Door breaks into a gallop like a long-legged horse. Tongues of fire flicker in the distance, the sun yearns, melting a thin film over your eyes. Door's gallop, which is virtually detached from the ground, seems so soft and pleasant that you put your head on one of the pillows of the couch and fall asleep. You wake up before reaching the base, lying on a pile of newly mown grass in a vast field. The shadow of the sunset has glided over the field that was warmed up by the sun during the day, oppressing the color of the field. In the short grass with tips as pointy as needles, the star-shaped flowers with yellow, bi-colored petals rustle in the breeze and avoid the sharp blades of scythes. While you were sleeping, Door reclined its tongue on the pile of grass, carried you down the couch, laid you down, and covered your back with great willingness. You hear voices next to you; you turn around. Door is playing in the grass with her most beautiful pup–a pup with a black coat and white paws–which we ate a few months ago. The naughty offspring suddenly skips and stands in front of the dog's wet nose. Until Door puffed and tapped on its nose with her paw, the puppy spun on one paw in one place like a true dancer and romped in the grass again. Sharp explosions are heard from the military base. On your feet. Alaaaaarm. The senior of the base is anxiously screaming to go inside the bunker. Door and the pup are petrified from the voices; they turn around and flee into the forest side by side. An AK-74 thrown over your shoulder, a bobbing helmet on your head, under the clatter of gunfire, you run to the sniper's nest through the underground passageway, relentlessly thinking about the little paw of the pup spinning like a top on Door's nose.

one

How could it fall? He was crouching down, even though he moved forward a little to pull up his pants, he thought, did he remember pulling up his pants, his body moving forward, or was he imagining it? He saw the protruding tip of the comb on the way to the bathroom, but it was not enough to slip out of his pocket, maybe on the way he combed his hair and didn't put it back properly, but he didn't have that habit, he always combed his hair in the morning, not in a long-winded sort of way, he simply brushed his hair forward. He had bought the comb in the city a year earlier; the saleswoman didn't have any change, so instinctively, without looking into his eyes, instead of a hundred drams, she put the comb in his hand. At that moment she was assisting a woman who was buying buckwheat and condensed milk. The woman buying buckwheat and condensed milk did not notice him buying the comb. She had bent her head over her bag, looking for her purse. What could the woman be doing now, who was she, did she have any children, what did she make with the buckwheat? It was nighttime. She was probably sleeping. But how was it that he picked it up from the floor and comfortably put it in his pocket, without thinking or, more precisely, without remembering; it was a comb, it fell, what do you do when a comb falls, you pick it up and put it in your pocket, what else? You're wrong. When he kneeled and pulled down his pants, he could still feel the presence of the comb in his cotton pocket, the tension in his knee joints hurt, he leaned his body forward, and right then he heard a sound. He didn't see the moment the comb fell. It was dark. He lit a lighter. It had fallen between his shoes, half of it in lemon-colored, tepid urine full of bubbles buzzing like bees. A shudder ran through his body. He held his breath. He felt weak tingles on his skin in different parts of his body. He held the crotch of his pants with one hand, crouched down, picked up the comb with his middle and index fingers, shook it, put it in the same cotton pocket, then pulled his shirt down, tucked it into his pants, buttoned up, and went out. The sound of the comb. Maybe the floor was full of urine, maybe it was heavy, maybe it had a hard surface, or was it the shoe that fell in the tepid urine, but he didn't move his feet before the comb fell, there's a possibility that he leaned on the balls of his feet when he lifted his heels, but his feet never fully detached from the ground. The vacant silence multiplied the sound of the splash; if only the sound couldn't be heard. He was confident that it had been dark inside, as dark as darkness stripped of memory. He lit the lighter and moved forward with small, careful steps. All the toilets were separated by cardboard walls, there was no one inside, he remembers it well, he chose the penultimate, the only more or less clean toilet bowl, he brought the light of the lighter to his legs, took up a comfortable position, pulled down his pants, and left his finger on the lever of the lighter. Everything fell into darkness again. From a distance, from a very far distance, together with the rustling of leaves, the sound of the comb splashing into the tepid urine becomes audible, he sees his own hand reaching out, picking up the comb from the floor, putting it in his pocket, going out of the bathroom, walking, standing near the tree and smoking, as if all of it was an indecipherable dream in which the most important episode was inaccessible, which no effort by his memory could restore. The abundance of oxygen brought him back to his senses. He looked at the noses of his muddy half-shoes and turned towards the base; before reaching the base, he stopped near the tree in front of the hospital, lit a cigarette, pleasantly played with the smoke between his lips, and nipped the filter with his teeth, envisaging in his imagination all the sweets he'd enjoy after being discharged. He had decided he was going to go to the *Halep*[9] shop and never come out again. He would eat so many sweets that day that in the end he would have to be taken to the hospital by ambulance. But his mind was on his favorite bar of orange taffy, and suddenly in his mouth he visibly felt the taste of smoke mixing with the sweet melting bar of orange taffy. Then he imagined a room suffused with a weak blue light shining through a window overlooking the street, and on the only bed of the room he imagined the naked, thin body of a girl, and he heard his own regularly pausing and insecure footsteps approaching the girl's body. Sucking in one last deep and long puff of smoke, he threw aside the half-burned filter and walked to the barracks. He didn't manage to sleep, his bed springs squeaked from time to time under his restless movements. When his body felt tired enough from his movements, he simply closed his eyes and moved from one darkness to another where it was safer. He woke up in the morning with a starting headache and a frozen body. Not participating in the military training, he took his towel and shaving supplies, and went down to the washroom. It was strangely silent, there were no soldiers at the sinks. He spread his legs wide, made himself comfortable in front of the cylindrical trough, arranged his supplies on the metal corner, and

---

9   *Halep* is a shop in Armenia started by Armenians from Aleppo, Syria, which exclusively sells Middle-Eastern foodstuff, including sweets.

vigorously began to wash himself with the virtually icy water dripping from the pipe. He collected water in his cupped hands and splashed it thoroughly on his neck, back, shoulders, armpits, chest, and stomach, reaching all the way down to his waist. He wiped his whimpering cold wet back and shiveringly shaved in front of a sharp shard of broken mirror. As he shaved, he always saw only one of his eyes and only one segment of his face in the sharp shard of broken mirror. His eye would freeze with short intervals in the shard, he would rivet his eyes at himself, then he would sadly squint his beautiful long lashes. He returned to the barracks, dressed with care, and took out of the drawer a piece of torn cloth blackened and coated with shoe polish, and with a few curt hand movements he brought shine to his half-shoes. Now he was ready for breakfast. He tried to remember how many times he had gone to the bathroom that year, he mixed up the numbers, but this one he would remember, he would constantly remember, because this one was the first and last time he went to the bathroom, because the comb fell, if it hadn't fallen and the sound had not been heard, if the lighter had not been lit, that whore would have never seen it and he would have never squealed to the whole battalion. At nights, in the hospital lobby, he carried out trials; he put the comb in the same pocket, pulled out the tip a little, crouched down, leaned his body forward, but the comb wouldn't fall, he would try again, brusquely shaking his body, but it wouldn't fall, he would continue his trials until sunrise, until his high temperature weakened him. His efforts were futile, even though the comb fell once. He pulled it out with his fingers, flung it to the ground, fell to his knees, and passed out screaming with helplessness. His mind would go numb from recalling the same episode day after day; for a moment he was convinced that the comb had not fallen, that the sound had never been heard, that no such thing had ever happened, and why won't it fall now? It won't fall at all, he cloaked himself in confidence, he believed that he did not light the lighter, that the lighter had not been on him, that he had not woken up that night, that he had not gone to the bathroom, that he had never even been in the army, that he had no home, no father, no mother, no brother, that he hadn't been born, then, however much he tried to counter his consciousness, the inescapable reality would bring him to his senses again, slowly, layer by layer. He pushed himself to sleep at length, hoping to deform the evidence somehow in forgetfulness. What had ever fallen out of his pocket? Nothing came to mind. In his imagination only the comb flew, the sound of the splash was heard, the light of the lighter and the sullied noses of his half-shoes were seen. But the comb was not in the tepid urine, it was a little away from it, but maybe he didn't remember it correctly, the puddle, in which half of the comb had fallen, had been formed from spit and urine, but who knows why it seemed to him, no, rather, he wanted it to have been formed from the clean spring water that streamed out of the forest. To make his trials more convincing, he took out four of the floorboards in his room with the short hospital spade, he pretended that it was a toilet bowl, he pulled down his underpants, held the comb between his index finger and thumb and urinated on its surface, then fearfully he brought it up to his nostrils; he didn't feel anything, it was scentless and colorless, but that was irrelevant; he had lost his wits over constant stress and exhaustion, and it was the traitor squatting in the last toilet stall who had seen everything through a crack in the cardboard wall, if only he knew that guy's name. Besides a few military booklets, porn magazines, the Constitution, and the Codes on the hospital bookshelf, there was a black-sleeved

Bible and a *Narek*,[10] coverless, more than half of it missing, swollen with humidity, and with shredded pages. To pass the time with something or other, he took the porn magazines, the Bible, and half of the *Narek* to his room, and he also took the only little flower in a clay flowerpot in the hospital lobby. He put the flowerpot with the flower on the window sill of his room and smiled; then he examined it for a long time from different corners in his room, gnawing his burning lips. He glued matchsticks together and, after a great deal of effort, he built a little house, but he had arranged the sticks so frugally that the little house, in its final appearance, resembled an ugly wrecked box. At night, lying in bed, he would prop up his head and back comfortably, take the Bible out of the gray drawer glued to his bed, and start to read it for the first time in his life, trying to focus and scatter his compulsive thoughts. But soon the gold cross on the black sleeve of the Bible would turn into a comb and the paragraphs would change into tepid puddles of urine, he would throw aside the book, bury his head under his pillow, and repeat to himself: I don't believe, I don't believe in God, I don't believe, I don't want to fool myself and in general I don't believe in anything, I've never thought about beliefs in my life, I don't have time for that, I don't need his help, I don't need his love and mercy. To him, the most interesting passages in the Bible were those about the life and miracles of Jesus Christ, which he did not believe in, but liked nevertheless. For hours he thought about how no one needed God besides fake clerics and tattered tramps begging in front of church doors, if he loved his son, he wouldn't leave him by

---

10   *Narek* or *The Book of Lamentation* is a tenth-century book of prayers written by the Armenian monk Gregory of Narek.

himself, he wouldn't invade earth, supposedly to say look at how generous I am, he himself would come instead of hiding anxiously behind his son, he wouldn't have had his only son killed in the name of human sin, and, leaving humans to fate's will, it was he himself who arranged for their destruction. Like an egoist, God had given man his own facial features and character, but he had not tried to create man. He had given people life, without love, and life isn't necessarily love, he had given a paradise where there were prohibitions, where the days passed by tediously and melancholically, and where Adam and Eve had probably become tired of making love under God's watchful eye, of eating and drinking, and of sleeping under the shade of trees. They had become sick of God's police control, because they were becoming more and more human with time, they were feeling the need for solitude and loneliness, and that's why they rebelled and searched for eternal love. Jesus was not God's son, if he had been his son, he would not feel, he would not pity people and he would not feel pain being crucified, they're lying, all books; there's not one honest book in the world, if someone decides to write a book, they decide to lie. Jesus's enemies wrote about Jesus. Jesus didn't know that he had come to save, he was convinced, when he lived among people, he was convinced that as a man he didn't want himself and people to suffer, to continually suffer, which meant to continually not understand, and he made the most modest decision of his life, he decided to save, but he didn't know that he would be crucified and that until the very end, with pounding heart, he would await another decision, he would await compassion and forgiveness, because with his crucifixion, his dream to save would also be crucified, the people would be left on their own, and he didn't want to leave them on their own, he didn't want to die, no one wants to die, not Cardinal either, or me, or Aram, or Black, or Taxi, or Mickey Mouse, or the commander, but compared to most, Jesus did not leave the path. He was not happy to die. Jesus's death was the saddest death in human history. From a young age, his mother taught him that prayers supposedly helped and God listened to the voice of the one praying and brought help, that it brought peace to the mind. But as time passed, peace moved farther and farther away from his mind.

He sadly felt like he was dying every moment and, renouncing the Bible, he would pick up and leaf through his old loyal friends—the faded pages of porn magazines and their intensely aroused naked bodies, baffling athletic poses, screams of pleasure frozen in the air, women's melon-like long, droopy, wide, very wide, sweet cracks, worn and discolored curly lips, rough and flashy images, the eyes of couples swallowed in pleasure—and he would feel a warm affinity with everyone, distancing himself completely for a moment, drowning in that charming world of eternally moving bodies where everything is open and agonizing. The New Testament of the military base's second battalion was the screening of porn movies on weekends, picked by him, for which the barracks were filled to the brim, soldiers even lay on the floor or perched on window sills, and whoever was anywhere came, the commanders of the rotating company together with the subordinate officers and the boys of the first battalion also joined, they came to revel high on weed, in a crazy mood, laughing and cursing left and right, but as soon as the movie started, the barracks would submerse in a deep silence; looking at the screen, everyone would shut up. Cardinal would have to scream, turn up the volume to the max, let's hear the voices loud, loud. Whoever was on duty would also be allowed to watch the movie through the crack of the door, but his eyes and ears had to be on the outside, if the commander, the chief of headquarters, or the military police suddenly appeared in the vicinity, he had to notify the rest. And before showing the movie, he would give a short emotional speech, introducing his chosen movie a little and justifying all of the good things about it and its points of interest. Most of all, he liked to tell about the life of the main actress, which he almost always made up, coloring her fate with great grief. Looking at Cardinal's sad face, uhm, uhm, uhm, hmmm-ing, he would coquettishly start his lecture, guys, Cardinal, the movie's actress, Seduel Schweinschedesch, uhm uhm uhm, well, the "schwein" she glued to her last name after going to Germany, she was born in Romania, when Seduel was five years old, she lost her father and mother in one day, their car fell in a valley and they died. And then an unmarried woman adopted her and raised her. Seduel was very beautiful, with long hair and blue eyes. Suitors killed each other for her, and her foster-mother, who was dying of poverty, took Seduel one day and sold her to one of the city's best-known rich pimps. Seduel suffered a lot. The pimp forced Seduel to sleep with just about anyone for no more than about a thousand drams in our currency. And then one day she disappeared, who knows how, who knows who got her a visa, she fled, and made it to Germany. They said that Seduel had slept with two thousand people in one week to pay for her travel cost, pahahahahaha-hahahahahahahahahahahahahahahahahahahahahahahahahahahahaha-hahahahahahahahahahahahahahahahahahahahahahahahahahahahaha-hahahahahahahahahahahahahahahahahahahahahahahahahahahahaha-hahahahahahahahahahahahahahahahahahahahahahahahahahahahaha-hahahahaha, the battalion exploded, but he hung his head and repeated to himself, Seda Seduk, Seduk, Seduuuuuuuk, what should I do Seduk, Seduk, my Seduk, I don't know Seduk, who knows what needs to happen for my Seduuuuuuuk, very quietly, so quietly that even in our imagination letters won't be legible, even in the fearful, doubtful loyalty of silence. The guys roared holding their bellies, and like big drops sitting on tin roofs after a heavy downpour their tears froze on their cheeks and on the corners of their lips. But suddenly Cardinal's voice thundered like a bullet ripping the air, fiiiiiiiiiiiiiiiiiiiiiiiiiiiiiiiiiiii ine, maaaaaaaaaaaaaaaaan, st O p, the man's telling a story, you idiots, A S T O R Y. Like monkeys seeing a snake, they all suddenly started, wiped their tears with handkerchiefs and sleeves, and shook their bodies. Continue, brother Truffaut, Cardinal said, encouraging him and lighting a thin Dutch cigar without looking at his face. Well, that's it, there's not much more to tell; it didn't take long for a well-known guy in the German porn movie industry to notice Seduel Schweinschedesch and invite her to play in movies. Seduel is now one of Germany's richest porn stars, she got married, she's got three children, one son, two daughters, and a really small ornamental horse the size of a dog. That's all. Okay, enjoy the movie. He pressed the play button and sat on the floor. The silence wasn't broken once during the entire film, no one annoyed their neighbor or unfamiliar soldiers from another company, everyone was spellbound, collectively and attentively following until the very end the passions exploding on the screen, the abundant water splashing off lone human bodies, the real and unreal groans of exposed instincts, the shrill and laughable moans done with special intonations for the camera, the exclamations in foreign languages that give allowance to wild pleasures that were not even shown until the end, the feeling that reflects the type, the happiness, the suffering, the pain, the cry for help. The only thing that brought together the military unit and all of its soldiers was porn movies; porn was the religion of the military unit and the military unit was its loyal apostle. But he got tired of everything, he got tired, he threw aside the magazines and books, then he picked up the Bible again during the day, reluctantly turned the pages, chose a prayer and read it to himself, and in the end he closed his eyes and waited; he decided that if God's help came, he would stand back, but he wanted to try, because it was interesting. Some time later, instead of God, the body of the girl would come, with the symmetrical wrinkles on the skin of a sort of plum that had fallen under a tree, feeble and projecting, with bones sticking out of her skin. The body would come, kiss his neck, and disappear. Then, hysterically, Bird would come, followed by a few cats tagging along, holding one of them, then it was Cardinal with his face pressed against the glass, hooooooooooooooooooooooooooooo ooooooooooooooooo-ing without moving his lips, then it was Mickey Mouse, a broom on his shoulders, running and burying himself in an eye. He remembered how one time, in the presence of the battalion guys, he pushed the vigorously sweeping Mickey, pushed him in dirt and spat in his face. His roar reverberated, he held his belly, swore and roared, exclaiming: sucky toilet cleaner, won't you sing for us, I promise, if you sing, I'll take you to the field with me, you'll see how I play football. Guys, you know, right, what his classmates did to Mickey Mouse? Do you know? If you don't, I'll tell you again, I don't mind. The guys would get annoyed, shake their hands, maaaaan, we know, we know, don't fucking talk our heads off, let this moron do his work. Mickey Mouse would nauseously get up crying loudly, pick up his broom, and get back to work. How did he sleep that night, did he sleep or not, did he think about sleeping at all, did he put his head under a blanket, does he have a blanket, or did he turn to the wall, did water flow out of his mouth on the pillow, does he have a pillow, I've never in my life been inside the woodshed, I don't understand, did Mouse cover himself with a blanket or not, did he sleep with his eyes open or closed, did he, like me, dream a few times of being in his own room, of lying in his own bed, but suddenly starting from happiness or wetness and finding himself in the woodshed abutting the mess hall curled up in a corner of his bed made with beams, burned oil containers, pieces of military metal, rims, wheels and branches, curled up with a fluttering heart and gaping eyes that were about to explode with stress? He pushes the little house of matches into a 10 cc syringe, walks up to the door of the hospital room, and lies down with his arms spread wide; the doctor's bony and moist fingers come out of the crack of the door, take the syringe filled with the little match house, and carefully push the needle into his artery; it's the dead who sleep with their eyes open; his eyes were open with the peculiar wickedness of frightening doll eyes without eyelids or lashes, his eyes have no inside or outside, if they are deprived of the world on the outside and of the mind on the inside, then they are at home, they have returned, abandoning destiny, lying at the military base on a squeaking bed with metal slats, in the deep sleep of a baby not yet born, suddenly his back is covered, the tip of his nose is pressed against the familiar dampness of the wall paper, the squeaking ends, his body melts into the bed, he smiles like a dreaming cat, because he can feel with his whole essence the long-lost spatial inevitability, he is at his house, sleeping in his bed where there is a window, a layer of light reflecting through the window, a soft, wavering bed and a warm, fuzzy blanket with lynx cubs, he sees how the blanket with lynx cubs rises and falls with his respiration, how his respiration has such a gentle rhythm and melting freedom, in his respiration he inhales all the ghosts and fairies, the little men with strange noses and clocks turn, I am breathing my breath, I am someone without an about, you know, I rise and fall on the world, I am the life that you have given to others, I have not been discharged, but I have returned home, I am sleeping in my room, in my bed, I have returned to breathe, I am breathing so that the world lives, so that everyone returns to their rooms where there are windows overlooking lights, to sleep in their own beds, under warm, fuzzy blankets with lynx cubs, which submit to whoever is alone, he is standing in their house, it's their house, with the same lively scent, the same ticking of the wall clock, which he often confuses with the workings of his heart, the hands of the clock are rooster heads with fiery combs, sparkling in the dark, when he was small, he would quietly get out of bed, softly tiptoe up to the clock, climb up the wall, reach the clock, go inside of it and sit on the comb of the rooster of the turning second hand, tick-tock, tick-tock, tick-tick-tock, the hand turned, turned, turned, tock-tock-tock, tick-tock, tick-tock, tock-tock, tick-tock, tick-tock-tock, tick-tock, tick-tock, he feels sleepy, he holds the head of the rooster with both hands and sleeps inside the clock until dawn, tick-tock, tick-tock, tick-tick-tock, the sound gradually fades and then vanishes into forgetfulness. Now he's standing in their house and he doesn't see the house, because, you'll recall, his eyes are dead, but he has strangely come, he doesn't see all of the suitcases in the closet, but he feels the leather and opens the locks, he doesn't see the long wall paper in the hallway depicting a dense forest, but the soft rustle of the forest strokes his cheek, he doesn't see the rough wooden doors opening with a creak, but he puts his fingers in the door; grandfather's chessboard is open on the desk; the blue ray of light shining through the mesh of the curtain glides over the square cages, dividing the space of the board in two, leaving one half in the dark and the other in clay-colored silence; the sad, fixed gazes of the pawns in the light are tense, full of pain from waiting; his body was so alone and stiff in one of the cages that it seemed as if it would explode wherever it'd be, breaching the notion of endless space; he's standing in one of the cages on the board next to the pawns, but he doesn't feel his presence, the borders of the cages, the unblinking ray of sun; he's one of the pawns, but he can no longer be distinguished from the others, he has the same tense gaze, the pain from waiting, but it's already impersonal and severed from his body and imagination; one pawn whose move belongs to the will of the board; here's the glazed tableware on the big table of the living room, the long-eared ringing glasses with sparkling stars from the refracted blue light reflecting through the window, through the glazed glasses objects come alive, melt, and bury themselves in striped wandering triangles, echoing sounds, and stretching to monstrous sizes, before narrowing and running after apparitions; through the glazed glass, reality unexpectedly dissolved and changed from moment to moment, for days he looked through the glass lost in himself and living a pleasant reality without happiness, because the world that opened up through the glass never repeated itself and now he's standing by his bed above whose head hang pictures of his favorite football players, he looks at him who is sleeping sweetly under the blanket with lynx cubs, then he weightlessly lies like he is lying, softly puts his head on the corner of the pillow, slides his right hand under the pillow, it's as if he has come to his own room, to never leave, the little clay soldier fallen in a field of yellow flowers in the distant past, to not forget the art of breathing; he's lost in water with joy, drops flow over his cheeks, lips, neck, and fall under the flowerpot on the window sill, he opens his eyes, it's the long military barracks, the air is heavy with the snores of soldiers, the metal bed squeaks monotonously under his restless tosses and turns; the subsequent deception and confusion of being asleep in his familiar room make him cry with his wide open, affected eyes, and cover his face with his blanket; let's see how the night passed for the un-self-loving mouse that had no desire to commit suicide, or to struggle, or to rebel, or to complain, or to run away from the military unit, or to kill someone, or to get killed, or to love or be loved, or to have friends, us guys even placed bets and chose the circumstances of his death, but Mickey, every day, at the break of dawn and in the evening, cleaned his toilets with a broom, with his head cast down, drowned in sweat, we changed the circumstances, and Mickey cleaned the toilets, no one in the world cleaned toilets like him, whatever happens Mickey will not leave the toilets, he won't sleep without cleaning, he doesn't think about anything other than cleaning toilets and all the other dirty areas, rotten mouse, chick of a slave, retard, only the last un-self-loving person won't hang himself with a rope and will continue to live in a woodshed like an animal, without friends, summer and winter wearing required gloves so that none of his fingers accidentally touch each other; with gloves that he does not take off, so that his skin does not accidentally brush against the skin of another soldier and that soldier gets soiled. The commander died saving money on Mickey. The commander could, if he wanted, spend a few thousand drams a month and bring people from the villages to work instead of Mickey Mouse, to clean the unit's toilets and all of the other dirty areas, and like that they would also earn a living and the boys wouldn't look for their next victim. But the commander triumphed, he kept that money swollen in his pocket, because there's the unit's Mickey, who had everything imaginable done to him by his classmates, and they had not forgotten, they had followed him to the base and had told the good guys of the battalion to stay away from him, to separate his plates and spoons, his food, his sleeping place, for the soldiers and officers to not talk to him, to not shake his hand in greeting. From that day on, Mickey was chased away from the barracks to the woodshed, he no longer entered the mess hall, immortal mouse, how does it not shoot to his heart, how does it not break his veins, how did he sleep that day when I debased him in front of the guys, my words probably rang in his ears and dreams, then again... what am I thinking? Falling in the bathroom was not unusual or dishonorable for Mickey, every day when he swept the toilets of the base his feet slipped and he fell. A week didn't go by that Mickey didn't get hit by one of the guys in the bathroom, that he wasn't pushed or made to sing, and if he didn't sing, we would beat him with a stick, then we would light the stick with gas so that not a single bacteria stayed alive on Mickey. But my comb fell in the bathroom and I picked it up, I wasn't allowed to, it slipped my mind that you couldn't pick up what had fallen in the bathroom, but how did I pick it up so negligently, no one is allowed to pick up what has fallen, even if it's a million dollars, gold, diamond, head, heart, eye, if it falls, that's it, you have to leave it and walk away, if it falls, it's lost. The one who saw it was probably one of Cardinal's whores, he had run and reached him, and Cardinal had needed a victim for a while already, he had not broken a soldier in the last few months, and if Cardinal continued to not break soldiers, his authority would weaken in the eyes of the troops. But I was his friend, although what friend for Cardinal, but what about my German and Russian porn films that I showed the whole base on weekends, if only they'd used that memory to forgive me? After the comb fell, Mickey's and my rank would be the same in the unit. I'll become the unit's substitute

Mickey Mouse. He would suddenly fly up like a ball, fall to the floor, and moan restrainedly. Then, when he came to his senses, he would lie down in his bed and recognizing, feeling with his fingers, licking the walls of his hospital room, he would feel safe again, he'd understand that he was still in the hospital, that the hospital is not the unit's bathroom, that the difference according to him was that right at this moment Mickey Mouse was cleaning the bathroom with a broom and bucket in his hand, while his chickenpox had just started, there's still time, he needs to stay in the hospital at all costs, he cannot leave its walls, as soon as he's discharged, he will immediately be shoved in a bathroom or other dirty area, that's what Cardinal had promised in front of the troops during the morning formation. He picked up half of the *Narek*, leafed through its pages, stopped on one of them, and read with a weak voice:

> My sins are frequent,
> But the humanism of your omnipotence
>   is victorious against everything;
> My vices are heavy and countless for my being,
> But for you they are very light and limited;
>
> What can a little darkness do to your God's light?
> How can a slight gloaming resist a ray of your size?
> How can the suffering of your crucifixion weigh against
>   the carnal unruliness of my feeble body?
> What, in your eyes, are...?

there was no one inside i didn't see anyone i stood in front of the door for a moment opened it with my foot and went in i didn't see anyone no one said hi get out of the way let me through if someone had said hi get out of the way let me through i would have seen him and heard hi get out of the way let me through the door closed and i was already inside i walked past the first stall there was no one if there had been someone i would've seen it i walked past the second one the third one the fourth one i was looking to see which one was more or less clean the light of my lighter went out at the fifth one it was somewhat clean but there was still the last one the very last one the fifth one didn't let me move on it pulled me like a magnet because it was clean i was alone in the bathroom i went in there was no one i lit my lighter and stepped forward there was no one behind me the door closed there was silence i didn't hear any voices i definitely remember the buzzing of flies the dripping from the rotten pipes i didn't smell any cigarette smoke the comb confused everything i wonder who hadn't liked the fifth stall that he left it clean i chose the fifth one it was so clean why did i choose the fifth one i didn't choose it i didn't think i was choosing it i had already chosen it before going into the bathroom i had chosen it instead of me they had already chosen me through a special ritual

...they will put a new broom in my hand and put me in a bathroom like Mickey Mouse, then they will have me clean all the other areas of the unit every day, they will steal from my hands the food and letters my mother sends, I'll move to the woodshed, I'll sleep next to Mickey, summer and winter I'll carry gloves, no one will greet me, they won't let me in the mess hall, I'll eat food like Mickey, every day at the same hour he stands by the window of the mess hall holding a silvery plate up to the sky with both hands, some time later the shutters of the window open, first a piece of bread flies out, then the cook's ladle sticks out and, without taking careful aim, it slowly tips over the watery potato and spills it, one part of it on his plate, the rest on his face and shoulders, the hot and watery potato sears Mickey's eyes, cheeks, neck, and all the soldiers and officers, every time they see this sight, dangle their legs and follow the movement of the ladle until the end, the pouring down of the stream of watery hot potato, the holding up of the silvery plate with both hands resembles a soldier waiting for manna sitting right under the window, on the ground, taking a spoon out of his pocket, sinking his teeth into the crust of the piece of bread and beginning his meal, and a soldier or officer standing not too far from him will automatically exclaim, enjoy your meal, little mouse, and Mouse, without looking at his face, without moving his gaze from his plate, his face practically dipped into the plate, answers with a smile, thanks, brother, please, let's eat, and his spoon trembles on the edge of his plate, if you put *Narek*'s book under your pillow...

it works miracles cures all pain how beautiful his lines are like an angry pointed feather weightless wild pounding meaningless quiet happy hopeless genius deep obscure clear i wonder if you had a lover Nar they say you lived in a cell your lines are addressed to your lover i know your manuscript is your letter to your beloved girl not to God the girl was probably the most beautiful walking in the tall grass with a transparent shirt a transparent body fffffffshsh-shshsh with long very long hair your long fingers probably touched the girl's shoulder stroked the girl's cheeks what gentle untouchable cheeks they are Nar her skin pale calling under her warm breath her half-dry lips with straight folds the folds are smooth your girl's breath flies out and detaches from the folds Nar how do you like it when your pinkie suddenly brushes against her breathing lips i wonder if you held

and loved each other missed and waited for each other i wonder if she brought bread and wine to your cell or did she get
scared of the color of the monastery's walls i wonder if she
combed your hair if her comb fell what would happen you're
a good guy Nar but you're not helping you're not showing
your power i've put your book under my pillow but it's not
working miracles it's not convincing me that i didn't pick up
the comb let me tell you that i did pick it up and everyone
already knows that i picked it up from where it had fallen i
shouldn't have picked it up from a forbidden area it is forbidden to touch anything that has fallen in human waste in
a dirty area i don't know in the bathroom in the other areas
adjoining the base's arsenal under the gate of the mess hall
in the woodshed where Mickey Mouse sits courteously Nar
our unit's untouchable the cleaner of dirty areas the king the
savior of soldiers is coming with a broom and bucket he saves
from the hands of the officers all the good and bad guys who
obstinately refuse to clean the areas Mickey saves everyone
from a huuuuuuuuuuuuge headache he's the only soldier
who hasn't held a gun or grenade in a year who hasn't fired a
single bullet and Super Mouse has only come up to the base
to clean and dig trenches he's the only guy who fearlessly
goes in and scrubs clean the forbidden area he himself is a
forbidden area starting from school number one thousand
no one has probably touched him besides his half-retarded
mother they made him keep a distance of a few meters once
in a while after work Mouse would lie on his back right in the
middle of the bathroom the sharp rays of sun shone through
the netted roof emphatically burying into his legs arms chest
eyes mouth he sprinkles crumbs of bread around himself and
on his body suddenly sparrows fill the room through open
passages in the roof and start to peck the crumbs i've seen it

secretly through the large cracks of the bathroom door i've
seen frozen in fear under the emphatic rays of sun shining
through the open passages in the roof lots of birds you can't
see Mickey's body for a moment it seems as if the sparrows
are pecking his body with my feet i'm kicking the door running in the flock of sparrows turned into a piece of rock flies
up with a gush of wind crashes against the roof scatters and
flies out through the passages Mickey Mouse is lying in the
same position sleeping with his arms and legs wide open and
his eyes closed and he hardly cared that he'd been exiled to
the forbidden area to work as long as there's work the more
the better the more he'll get tired the deeper he'll sleep but
the turn has come to me i'm the next one everyone waited a
long time the troops the commander of the unit forgive me
your beloved girl is so beautiful Nar goodbye my brother
take care

    This book in my voice instead of my person,
    As I, must always cry out,
    Spread that which was covered,
    That which was secret, it must disclose,
    Bewail my deeds with grief,
    Bring to the fore what was forgotten,
    What had been invisible and imperceptible,
    By divesting manifesting,
    Proclaiming my guilt,
    Propagating what was buried in the depths,
    Tell of my sins and display secrets in their purest form...

let

      the

          light

                        of
                                your
                                    stamp
        unite
            with
        the
            form
                now
                    always
                        forever
                            and ever

amen

    the

        stamp

            of

                your

                    light

forever

unite

with

the

form

through

the

comb

the

stamp

of

your

light

inject

my

path

I have money doctor

                I'll pay

                    five

thousand

drams

for entrance

       your

           family

                will

send

you

more

                bring

me 10 cc

syringes

bring them

                              with needles

in different sizes
   the stamp
     of your
     light

your arm on the door

between the messy

places

inject

the path

of

m

y

en

trance

doctor

That day he was sitting all by himself at a table in the mess hall and he didn't notice that his plate, spoon, and fork had been changed. He was eating a boiled egg with a trained appetite, regrettably gulping down tea over it, now and then casting a glance at the bald head of the soldier sitting at the table across from him. He went out to the courtyard and walked to the smoking shed. Soldiers who walked past him did not greet him, they turned their heads and grunted under their breaths. Ignoring their behavior, he went into the shed, leaned against the slats, took a cigarette out of his pocket and lit it. Taxi was standing a few meters away shelling wet melon seeds, collecting the kernels in his elastic cheeks like a beaver, and examining him with interest, then with the help of his tongue and teeth, he would separate the kernel of the melon seed from its shell. His jaw, with its flexible and crude to and fro motions, was constantly working. Feeling Taxi's transparent shadow on his back, he turned around and smiled widely. Taxi, you graze like a horse every day, pity your cheeks. He laughed loudly, waiting for a laugh in reply. But the corners of Taxi's lips froze without opening, and he angrily shoved his hands into his pants pockets. No, really, are you serious? I'm supposed to believe this? He hesitated for a moment, not getting Taxi's tone of voice. He didn't like that brazen, for him surprising, completely serious response. He measured him from head to toe with a disgusted, stern look on his face, he wanted to curse, but he didn't get to. Did you pick up the comb from the bathroom floor? Taxi lashed out. In the beginning he didn't understand the meaning of what he had heard, his brain froze. His fingertips felt cold and stiff. The comb was probably made of diamonds, eh? Taxi roared. That's why you couldn't stop yourself, you bent over and picked it up. He stopped breathing, for a moment he uttered gurgling sounds, it was as if a lamb was being slaughtered under his feet, he wanted to knock his face against the silver rim of the ashtray. The muscles in his face tightened and his heart changed rhythm. Aaaaaaaaaaaaaaaaaah, take it easy, from now on, you'll have fun in the bathroom and those other places with that sucker Mickey Mouse. With his eyes he looked for a big rock, a metal pipe, a piece of wood, a nail, he wanted to kill Taxi, to smash his head in with a rock, to ram the metal pipe in his eye, to pull it out and ram it in again, to rip him to pieces, but he was already exhausted. It was as if his internal organs gained the weight of rocks every passing moment, he didn't feel whose hand rose, who took off his hat, whose body collapsed on the seat; he had become weightless, his eyes had popped out of their sockets and were skipping on the roof of the tent. Taxi had not left, but he was no longer noticeable, he had approached him from behind and had spat on his neck and back, shelling melon seeds. One of the good guys of the battalion sitting next to you saw how you picked up the comb from the floor, there's no reason Cardinal should doubt him, you hear, man, Taxi continued, spitting the shells on his close-shaved head. You still keep the comb in your pocket, at least throw it out now, but his voice was already distant, very distant, because he turned to dust in the smoking shed; in the back of the mess hall, near the library, in the training area, he totally lost his sense of self, the vital ability to perceive his own body; he could only see…

he sees him in front of him his other his build the length of the wall of the mess hall the door of the woodshed the endless row of windows dust balls soldiers half-shoes bread on shoe polish in the sun when we ate just for fun the milk bile bile horribly bilious sticking to the roof of your mouth like pitch was simmering on the fire in a pot drink it and let your mouth your palate completely burn drink and die die broken toys mom cleaned them up and kept them i broke the car's two wheels melted them on the fire of the gas at university i would go down under the pass to pick out a present for you but where were the teeth someone had hit the teeth hard and smashed them then the prostitute had cried had apparently cried he knows she had feelings she cried when she lost her teeth because they were beautiful she had had a beautiful row of teeth a fragile gentle girl without bones on her face there were deep scars they had torn her with a knife they had probably wanted some but she hadn't given them any they had left cuts on her skin with a knife and she had cried again she was probably sensitive sensitive don't think that there's a completely insensitive person in the world even corpses are sensitive breathlessness is the matter of breathing but listen listen forget all that listen there was something going on with that girl like a freckled person she spun in the free space of her empty soul she touched the walls in her soul she changed her orbit organless how exciting to have just one organ just one crack allowing all the world's wheels through one crack but she was sad inside she didn't feel anything the pain inside was a lot she perpetually sunk deeper and deeper in the emptiness the emptiness that is time without organs time without the weight of emptiness that is a compass not a watch unmoving hand but the freckled person was there like a snowflake with the tenderness of a sharp needle the freckled one the girl's body when it was transparent completely alone in the emptiness the freckled one swayed her little head well in her body that for me was the same soul again the same and let me tell you that the girl had had a doll when she was a child and she had been a child at the time she had two little pigtails with chubby little hands on the little hand they had kissed a beautiful little birthmark many good people the birthmark on the little hand with red dots in the dress she was wearing her mom had walked her around the courtyard and the little girl had seen a little boy had run up to him and kissed the little boy's cheek but the boy had frowned and like a piglet had scratched the girl's crooked nose and they had stood there together crying sadly sadly two cute babies a little girl and a little boy who didn't know whether they would grow up or not they didn't know that they were living now because what they know now at this moment is life well yeah for them without any knowledge life's name is loving very much loving very very much which they can't resist she walks among the clothes and shoes she enters under soles she rubs herself against the nails of the soles she remembers what she was thinking she sees irene's shoulder is leaning against the donkey's leather the donkey's leather is leaning against irene's shoulder the surface of her nail touches the donkey's leather letting out dripping sounds the surface of the nail touches the donkey's leather letting out dripping sounds Irene wants to understand why in her interior space it takes so long to go without knowing the beginning and the end of a day why he and irene don't go to the mess hall to eat why his friends aren't walking irene why he thought isn't irene going to eat why isn't irene washing dirty ireneireneirene three of them joined together irene doesn't need to wash herself why aren't the officers calling her why aren't you getting thirsty he doesn't buy cigarettes he follows her home without getting tired he waits for irene patiently she's indifferent to him even though she knows that he comes home always comes home why does he come quietly you live repeating her footsteps at the unit there are no yous there are irenes just like he stood in front of the hospital door knocked on the door after some time the doctor sleepily opened the door and said what

I want to see Aram

You can't see Aram, the chickenpox quarantine hasn't been lifted yet. I have to see him, for one minute, I have to see him, I need to tell him something. Don't you understand, soldier, I said you can't. No, I can, please. Oh man, you're not crazy, are you? What do you want? Let us sleep! One minute, I need to tell him something. Oh maaaaaaaaaaaan, are you out of your mind? What's your battalion? The second. The second? Then what do you want from Aram? You want to talk to your friend to see if you can move to the first battalion? Be honest. No, me and Aram used to live on the same street, give me one minute to tell him something and go, please, can I? Oh maaaaaaaaan, fiiiiiiiine, you're driving me nuts, come, come, go. The doctor in the dirty lab coat barely holding on to the door, rocking on his feet, pulls to one side and let's him in. Go straight down the hall, turn a sharp left, he's in the last room, as you walk loudly repeat, I'm in the hospital, I'm in the hospital, hospital, chop-chop, move it, I'd better see you back here in a minute. He's walking and loudly repeating, I'm in the hospital, I'm in the hospital, in the hospital, in the hospital, hospital, hospital, hospital, hospital, hospital, hospital. Aram was lying with a high fever on the only iron bed in the patient room. They were from the same neighborhood, they lived on different floors of the same entrance in the same building on Frik Street. He never befriended Aram in their courtyard, but one of his happiest moments at the base was when he found someone familiar, someone close to him among all the rookies who had come to serve. Aram burned in his fever with wandering eyes, practically unconscious, with the moist respiration of a dying man. He sat on the iron edge of the bed, on the sheet hardened with dirt. With the palm of his hand, he stroked his friend's cheek with green spots. I wonder if you're happy, my brother, you don't know, either, do you? You're kicking the bucket, Ar, kicking the bucket, I mean what's the point of you living, didn't you go through chickenpox as a kid, didn't your mom rub antiseptic on your face, on your back didn't she blow cold, pleasant cooling air, fwooooooooooooosh, whooooooooooosh, didn't she separate your cup, your plate, your spoon, didn't she stop your friends from hanging out with you, didn't she stop you from going down to the courtyard? They imprisoned you in loneliness at home, didn't they? The same plate, the same spoon, the same cup, their sad immobility, the same frozen drip of the wall clock, the same fat fly repeatedly knocking against the window like a lunatic, on the window sill the flower in the clay flowerpot with a rust-stained fork thrust under it, neither the dark, nor the light, nor the sun, nor the moon in the responseless ascetic room, in an almost plain mood, and you, who are listening to your family's exchanges through the closed door with longing, you're listening to how their dinner spoons, plates, and cups clink and clank synchronously. You want to catch their every uttered word, their arguments, their grave analysis of everyday problems, the moment your mother throws out the garbage and peels potatoes, the flushing of water out of the tap, then you ask her to at least draw the curtain, to open up the view in the window. Lying in bed, you see how bluish snowflakes fall from the sky, snowflakes that look like sharp, ruffled feathers from a distance, you see that and silently point your finger at the snowflakes, then you hear children in the courtyard, all of your friends' joyful exclamations; they're probably throwing snowballs at each other, running, falling in the snow, the snow hits their face, sits on their eyelashes, melts in their mouth, then they probably ride sleds; sleds with red green blue yellow slats. The shrieks of their games and happiness, their running, their slipping on ice, the sled, the taste of snow, everything has converged in the flakes, which fall from the sky with the melancholy of irreversibly cast-out white angels. But you're alone, caressed by the curly dry wrinkles of the sheets; you're closed to everyone, but not to the window, on the other side of which is life, an apparition that inexplicably emerged gently and painfully, that you don't know who gave or why it was given, but you know definitely that it's not only to live and die, not only to suffer and enjoy, not only to excite and disappoint; it's something else; it, it is something else; truth, without which it would be impossible to express oneself, is an exceptional possibility to express oneself; life is a child's little finger pointing at snowflakes–and in his eyes, sparkling delight. But now you're not allowed to join the kids in the courtyard, because in this same life people get sick and infect others, and you need to be cured, if you get up now and go down to the courtyard, many of your friends will flee if they see you, they'll be scared to touch your body, your clothes, their mothers will strictly forbid them to hang out with you, get used to sadness, you have no other choice, get sadness used to your body, convince it that from now on you'll be sharing life; delight in your sadness. Aram opens his eyes wide, his lips are twitching, you want to kill me? You shouldn't have come, they'll catch you, crush you, come late, the doctor will be sleeping. After his breathless, barely quavering sentence, he completely held in his chest for a moment like a spring and then with a click opened it up, letting the collected cough in his lungs burst out, shaking his body. Aram deeply moaned in pain, closed his eyes, and never knew that his friend greedily swallowed his barely expelled contagious droplets of water, then ran his finger down the guy's sweaty arm and forehead, then raised it to his mouth and licked it. Up to the moment he was leaving, he barely resisted the big desire that had grown in him to kill his friend, he wanted to strangle him, not with his hands, but by putting some sort of hard thing on his face and pressing it down. For a long time he looked with his head tilted at his friend's thin neck, at the blue vein running through his neck. For a moment it seemed as if the blue vein running through his neck was the world's most beautiful river. Goodbye. He went back the same way he had come, this time repeating out loud I'm not in the hospital, I'm not in the hospital, I'm not in the hospital, I'm not in the hospital, I'm not in the hospital, even though the doctor had not demanded it a second time. In a dream, completely naked, he had appeared in a room where faceless men in long white coats were melting silver and looking at him silently. They were standing right in the middle of the room next to a rusty bed. Slowly, with hesitant steps, he approached the rusty bed, lay down and supinely continued to follow them gradually surrounding the bed. Suddenly one of them cut his chest open with a scalpel in his hand, and another sunk a fork in something important and fatal for him, but he didn't see what it was. Then they brought a cup filled with boiling liquid silver to the dark opening in his chest and poured it down–he didn't feel any pain; they slowly glided the cup over his face, held it to his open mouth, and tipped it over. The boiling stream of liquid silver sizzled down his mouth. To the end he saw and felt his melting head, even the composition of his vocal chords, but didn't hear his scream.

His temperature had risen sharply in the evening, and his body felt like it had been beaten with a blunt object. At night, they put him in a bag, dragged him to the hospital, tossed him on a bed in a patient room and left. There was no question about the diagnosis: it was newly sprouted chickenpox. The permanent doctor of the hospital, who had a narrow frame, square mouth, arms and legs as thin as a spider's and inconsistent with his body, muttered and complained to the commander of the battalion as he filled out the hospital register that this idiot came a few days ago, I wouldn't let him in, I said you can't, there's a risk of infection, but he insisted, you could've told him a thousand times, it's the same cretin. He was all by himself at the hospital, all three patients had healed and were released, and who knew why new ones weren't brought in. Maybe I'm the last patient in the world, he thought and in a way rejoiced that at least in this case the exceptional precedent would work for him. After prescribing an antiseptic, a few orange vitamins and pills in the beginning, the doctor came twice a day, checked up on his health, then walked out down the hall, whistling and playing with a matchstick between his teeth. He locked the heavy hospital door behind him with a few strong locks, firmly pushed it a few times from the outside, knocked on it, and left. If the task force sent some food during the day, the doctor would open the door, put the tray on the floor, then quickly close the door again, not forgetting to push and knock on it a few times. Then the visits diminished. He would come once every three days, drunk, with the wrinkly and spotty skin of a newborn, he would open the door of the room constantly yawning from unsatiated sleepiness, lean against the jamb, and always ask the same question: you want me to pull your tooth? He wouldn't say anything, he would turn to the wall and pull the covers over his head. He was annoyed. Are you annoyed? Man, I'm saying it for you. You don't want it, I won't pull it, eh. The pain of the chickenpox had enveloped his body. His skin dipped in antiseptic moaned from the stinging burns. He was cautious about appearing in a mirror, even though he thought that a mirror would be able to handle it and not show his greenish face saturated with unpredictable emotions. On the very next day, he had given the doctor all the money he had on him, asking him to bring 10 cc syringes with needles in various sizes. The doctor brought the syringes the next day, but he requested that he add money to it, even threatening that he would release him from the hospital before his time. He offered the silver cat's head on a black string hanging from his neck, but on one condition, that the doctor, if necessary, whenever he wished, would inject him. Shaking his shoulders and yawning, the doctor put the silver head in his pocket and agreed to the condition.

He had fallen apart after reading his brother's letter multiple times. He had started to forget his brother's features, most of the time he invented them the way he wanted to, he scratched something on a piece of paper, lips, a moon-like nose, but sometimes he would get his grandfather's face and he'd remember that his brother couldn't stand it when he was compared to his grandfather, he always got pissed off and left. Unlike him, his brother never dreamed, he always worked hard, confidently, without having a single goal in life. He was always busy with seriously important work, he wanted to start a dough factory, then a sour cream production company, a kennel for stray dogs, he wanted to be the first to import high-quality foreign pesticide that cures grape vines. He was constantly changing his workplace, complaining that people don't appreciate his dedication and work, they don't appreciate his real strength and talent as an employee. His brother was convinced that whatever he did was outstanding, gifted, and exceptional. Lying in bed at night, they would talk for a long time, in the beginning only his brother would talk, long, with broken thoughts and short meaningless stories, then he would dream, putting his hands under his head, and start excitedly with glistening eyes. His brother would genuinely feel thrilled by his seriousness, twitching the muscles in his face and making himself more comfortable in bed. And he would talk with excitement, getting up at the same time, emotionally pacing around in the dark room, looking out the window, smoking, lying down again, then anxiously asking for the time, talking about a special breed of guinea pig that can recite poetry. He took the opportunity to try to describe precisely in detail the essence of his dream, not leaving out a single minutia, moment, image, experience, he explained his dream's inner and outer workings, showed the easiest way to reach it, he felt worried and overwhelmed by expected difficulties, but in the next moment he burned with new hope and, if he made his dream come true, he definitely knew the first step. Straight from the airport in Paris, he would go to a scarf shop and buy a long, very long scarf for his beloved girl. And what if you go in the summer? His brother snorted, barely able to resist laughing. Doesn't matter. People wear scarfs in the summer, too. I know. So, then, what are you going to do in Paris? His brother continued. Well, in the beginning I'll steal, together with the Arabs, I'll steal jeans, phones, and sell them at a cheap price at a black market. Hey, heeeeeyyyy, you'll get caught. Even better, the jails in France are like paradise, with Chinese and Taiwanese cuisine, brilliant conditions, I googled it, I watched prison guards apologize every two seconds for no reason at all. And then? His brother laughed. What then? Then I'll come out of prison, I'll get a job, I mean, I don't know, I'll do something, I won't do nothing, the important thing is I'll be in Paris, I'm thinking I'll go to an old lady's, I'll look after her, I'll take care of her, and she'll adopt me, she'll leave her entire fortune to her caregiver, her only son. You really put a lot of thought into it, I have nothing to say, you've drawn out your path, good for you, you'll get there, don't worry about it at all, okay fine, it's going to be light soon, if mom wakes up, she'll skin us both, good night. Good night. But he couldn't sleep. Until morning, he continued to dream and dream; he kept repeating to himself that everything would change there, because I won't be here, I'll be there, where it's different; the streets are different, the colors of people are different, the languages are different, the water is different, the taste of food is different, circles of friends are different, even dreams will be different, happiness and pain will be different, diseases will be different, the sun and moon will be different, dawn and dusk, rudeness and hardship, windows and doors, love and hope. That difference would let him become that which he couldn't make one of a kind here, and he would become, definitely become, but what and how, he didn't know. His brother thought a lot about their talks and meetings, he was convinced that his brother belonged to that number of dreamers whose dreams never came true; they have no connection whatsoever with life and reality; those are not dreams, those are youthful glimmers of adventure and enthusiasm, some glistening shards that remain just as incomplete in some doughy imagination. He thought about what kind of a brother he was for that kind of a dreamer, life doesn't forgive, it hurls you out of the limited confines of reality. Deep down he was scared for his brother's future, let's say, when he met a homeless beggar on the street, for a moment he'd believe that the same fate awaited him, because he saw the same like-minded wretchedness of glistening shards in the beggar's and his brother's eyes. To dream is to choose the shortest path to death, his brother thought and, scattering his thoughts, swiftly crossed the street. And he, besides dream, did nothing at all to make his dreams come true, it was like his inner belief was so strong that sooner or later he would have the world working for his dream, it would attract like a magnet, it would bring all the necessary workings and secret events, and fate would take on all the responsibility, because his job was merely to dream and like a responsible schoolboy he did his job every day, and he thought that dreaming needed exercise like a muscle, he even set aside a special time every day to dream, from 7:00 to 8:30 p.m., he absolutely had to lock himself up somewhere–in a room or at a cafe in the city—and start to dream, then, when that time was up, he would go back to life with the same rhythm of the day. Like that, he discovered for himself all the magic of cafe life and for the first time he started to pay attention to people. But his brother left for Paris. One day, he came in out of breath, gathered everyone, kissed them one by one, and said that the French ambassador had issued him a visa. Right at that moment he wished his brother dead, he wanted to see his heart suddenly burst open, to see him collapse on the floor and writhe to death. He hated the fox that had secretly stolen his dream, its cold-hearted, hideous mien that worked in silence, and he hated himself for voicing and disclosing his dream, and he hated the feeling that from now on his impressions of Paris would be directly linked to his brother's life, and little by little he understood that if he continued to dream about Paris, he would no longer picture with his own eyes and his own imagination the city, its streets, cafes, museums, suburbs, sex shops and newsstands, wines, scarves and chocolate stores, flickering neon lights, but he would see only those places where his brother had been, he would analyze only those things that his brother had done, he would spend time only with those people that his brother had met, he would buy the scarf that his brother had picked, not for his beloved girl, but for his substitute French or Croatian girlfriend. You could hear his loud sobbing at the airport. He had wrapped his curled-up, now and then shaking body around his brother and was bawling like a child. Everyone watching the goodbye was affected, they tried everything to calm him down, to have him take heart, they brought him a glass of water, urged him to take at least one sip. He raised his head, cast a sad glance at the glass, turned it down with closed eyes, and put his head back on his brother's shoulder. His mother, sister, even his brother's friends stroked his thin hair, patted his back, whispered kind words in his ear; he wouldn't calm down. He didn't see the plane take off, he had fallen asleep exhausted, and his lip quavered.

It was imperative that he read his brother's letter once a day and put it back under his pillow:

"Hi, bless your heart, how are you? How's the army? I moved to the fishermen street, I'm caring for a grandmother over eighty, I live at her house. Bro, you're almost done, cope with it, one year will go by fast, you'll come to Paris, by the time you get discharged, your visa issues will be solved, I don't work on those things anymore, you probably remember the jeans store I was telling you about. The Bosnian grandmother doesn't pay all that bad, I'm not bothered, I clean, I do laundry, and I bathe her once every other day. Bro, no one here is ashamed of the type of work they do, what's important is that there's work. Listen, let me tell you something interesting, it'll make you feel better. So, this grandma, Elena Bukijich, bought a goose about seven years ago and lived with it like a dog, the way people keep a dog, and when she was completely bedridden, she turned the care of the goose over to me and raised my wage, asking me to take care of her too after she died, and made me swear that no matter what happened, I would never kill the goose and I would never eat it. The name of the goose is Luke, but, well, since I'm the one taking care of Luke now, I've decided to add a new name to its existing one—Vacho. Luke-Vacho. Me and Luke-Vacho didn't get along in the beginning. Luke-Vacho has an arrogant and vain character, it suddenly got annoyed and completely refused to eat anything. I begged and pleaded for hours, I asked for forgiveness so that it would eat something, so that it wouldn't die, so that the grandma wouldn't curse me out of anger and throw me out, but little by little we came to under-stand each other and got along, whether we liked it or not. I've told Luke-Vacho a lot about you, I showed it your picture, when you come to Paris, I'll leave its care to you, all day you'll walk around the streets and parks of Paris, everyone will look at you surprised and smile. I take Luke-Vacho out for a walk twice a day, I really like its collar, you'll like it, too, it's leather, light, with beautiful patterns. As soon as the Seine appears from a distance, Luke-Vacho gets very excited and starts to waddle away, and I'm barely able to keep up with it. Luke-Vacho is an intelligent goose, if only you saw how carefully it crosses the street, attentively following the changing colors of the traffic light. Things like that, my brother, I tell you again, don't worry, everything will be fine, if there's internet at the base, send me a letter to my e-mail, I'll wait impatiently and don't forget to look after yourself, dress warmly, don't catch cold. I talked to our homefolk a few days ago, they're well, they're all waiting for your return, but Paris and I, for YOU. Goodbye."

He takes a piece of paper and a pencil, and tries to reply to his brother's letter. I picked up the comb, I can't come to Paris. He shreds the paper and takes a new one. The comb was in my pocket when I went into the bathroom, then it fell on the floor, and I picked it up, I picked up the comb from the floor, I'd forgotten, I definitely remember, that the comb fell far from the tepid urine, even though it was probably wet, I forgot I was coming to Paris...

New paper.
You can't pick up what has fallen on the bathroom floor, there's no need to work on a visa. He picked up a new piece of paper. Had the sound of the comb not been audible, the whore sitting in the last stall would not have noticed...

New paper.

It was the lighter's fault, a thousand times you said don't smoke.

The pieces of paper cover the bed like flakes of snow.

He woke up every day at dawn when the sun's thin ray, skimming the tree bark, shone through the window, burning his cheek and a little bit of his lip. He would get out of bed, stand in front of the only barred window in the room, stick his head through the bars, and look for a long time at the tree trunk that rose very close to the window and that was his only outside. One day in bed, he saw how he got out of bed and shuffled up to the window, he saw how his head inserted itself between two bars, the tree trunk intently looked into his eyes as if someone from behind, gently holding his forearm with both hands, raised his arm, pulled it out of the bars with care and pressed his fingers against the trunk. For a long time he caressed the shadowy bark, which was warm and vigorous like summer rain. He plucked a piece of the tree trunk and went inside, took a 10 cc syringe out of the drawer, then put the piece of bark in it, placed the longest needle on the syringe, and lay on his bed. The doctor came at night. As soon as he heard the sound of the hospital door, he jumped out of bed, went up to the door of the patient room, and sprawled on the floor with his face to the plastered ceiling. The doctor's erratic and dull footsteps moved forward down the hallway up to his room. He had closed his eyes and was thinking about the flower in the flowerpot, he was thinking whether the flower can hear human words, do flowers even have a sense of hearing, do they need sounds, the surf of the sea, the chirping of birds, the moaning of humans? Where is the heart of a flower? The doctor stood in front of the door, but didn't open it, didn't knock on the door; he was breathing heavily with a wheeze, you could even hear the beating of his heart. The hearts of the flower and doctor. You never hear the flower's, but the doctor's was beating like crazy. Scared heart.

hello
hello

Are you taking your pills, your vitamins? How are you feeling? Do you want me to pull out your tooth? I'm taking them, I'm a little feverish, no, you don't need to pull out my tooth, leave it there. Well, look, I'm saying it for you, if you want, I can pull it out, I have the tools with me, they're good tools—new, with pain killers—don't be afraid, you won't feel any pain. No, doctor, my tooth doesn't hurt, thanks, you don't need to pull it out, I wanted to ask you something, do you remember our agreement? Yeah, I remember, tell me what you want, what am I supposed to do now? I've filled a 10 cc syringe, I prepared it, I want you to inject me, will you inject me? I'll inject you, but this will be the first and last time, after this, whenever you want, my hand will come to inject you, I don't feel like coming to the hospital every day, I work at the city hospital, I have very sick patients. You know everyone in the battalion is talking about you, I'm telling you so you know, the guys are in a very bad mood, if you have a way, call your family and let them know, let them move you to another base, the way you are now, here, you won't last long, if you want, give me your home number, I'll call them and inform them, I won't tell them the details of the incident, I'll just say that I'm a kindhearted person, the only doctor of the base, that all the guys are unhappy with the base, they want to move to another base, that the military staff lead the soldiers to suicide and major inner conflicts, that the commander is nothing more than a half-crazy, ignorant prick, supposedly with a heroic past, but the guys found out that he hadn't even taken part in a single battle in the war. The commander beats, humiliates, and tortures disruptive soldiers in front of everyone, trying to discipline them by using his own methods. But God forbid someone falls into his hands on drugs–he'll finish them. But he's made friends with the good guys of the base, for instance, he shoots up with Cardinal Gugo, they bring prostitutes from the city and have orgies all night. You'll probably remember when he found out you screened porn films on Saturdays and Sundays for the battalion, he called you to him, your heart stopped, you thought this is it, you're living the last moments of your life, now he'll shoot off your head, but lo and behold he was encouraging you for being able to keep the guys busy and unwind them on weekends, he demanded a copy of a DVD with the best porn videos of your choice on it; though, no, I won't tell your mother about this, I'll just explain that the base of our unit is dangerous to lives, that they are continuously subjected to the enemy's diversion attacks, it would be good if they moved their son for a little money to a more peaceful base, huh, what do you say, you fell asleep, oooowwwwww, you died, what happened to you, are you listening? Doctor, inject. His thin, very thin hand slips under the door of the patient room, picks up the syringe filled with tree bark from the ground and, driving the needle into his lung, injects him; what happens when water the color of fish fins flows through a river and takes with it the range of rolling seaweed, rowboats of leaves falling from trees that crash against beachrocks; life sleeping in bed covered in leaves instead of a blanket, the purling river falls silent, you wake up from a deep sleep, you get out of bed and walk, you pass by the window, you stand by the tree, after a short pause you embrace the tree with both arms, put your head against the bark, then you raise one hand, you open your palm wide and place it in the strong ray of sun, the familiar sound of branches shaking like crazy, the shivering rustle of leaves, the palm of your hand brimming with mulberry fruit, the fruits falling from the tree on the mulberry sheet, here and there flowery and unused pieces of cloth; the cloth with big coarse stitches and threads resembling black snake hatchlings looked like a group of islands fragmented together that in the course of years had been covered with a layer of mulberry hue from the sticky fruit juice and the golden fruits falling from the branches shaking like crazy from the crazed tree, like goat teats with long, white, big, greenish, baffling hues. You've turned your face to the rays peering through the foliage, the mulberry leaves flutter from the openings of the fine meshing, which beat against the foliage and lightly press against the edges of the green rowboats, filling up the veins and cooking the sweet mulberry fruits; the clustered bunches of lights through the leaves are sparkling little suns in the dark shadows; you pluck the white juicy fruit, put it on your tongue and squash it between your tongue and palate; you gargle the juice in your mouth; you feel the flow of the sun's brooklet in your soul; the taste of the sun; you eat that life-giving frame, which bestows its existence on every single mulberry fruit; you close your eyes and it's as if drops are raining under the sky's lavish sun, the fruits touch your head, your shoulders, the tip of your nose, your cheeks; your lips; a few of the fruits, brushing over your eyelashes and slipping under your shirt, fall into your lap; your smile grows wider and wider, it's as if someone independent of your will is smiling instead of you, because this is the first time in your life that you have been trusted to hold one end of the mulberry cloth, and you are holding it will all the strength of your body and all the responsibility of your little mind; you're holding the end heroically and you turn around the tree carefully, constantly looking down in front of your feet, terribly afraid of even the most inconspicuous pebbles falling under your soles; you want to appropriate the steps of the others in an instant, trying to memorize the movements of their feet and bodies, but you can't follow from memory, because you are different, your steps are different, the bloodless scabs on your skin, your knees disproportionately sticking out, different knees, your legs tremble with emotion, different emotion, a gaze looking at the sun, a different sun, then everything yellow, a different yellow; to keep step with everyone else, but better than everyone else, excel at your next unrepeatable step, restrained, gentle, and untrembling, so that you don't accidentally drop that end of the cloth, and you don't hang your head, so they trust you again next time; right at this moment, as you hold the end of the mulberry cloth tightly in your hands, you are given an exceptional opportunity to feel the importance of your presence for the first time in your life; the leaves of the branches bent by the harvest rustle from the terrible shakes, the tree branch has as much rhythmic fury as the trembling of the little boy's matchstick arm; you can hear the unrepeatable melody of fruits hitting the cloth; glglglglglglglglglgl every time a branch is shaken, the fruit that hits the cloth is welcomed with shrieks of joy; the fruits are falling, falling, some of them on the ground, some of them on "Jori's" skeleton, which has been in the courtyard since the day you were born, they flip over, fly up, roll down, feeling, caressing, kissing the surface of the cloth, piling up on top of each other, waiting for grandma's hands already dead long ago, incomparably long hands for her short height, with savagely tender, lively fingers, black twirling capillaries under the skin like wiggling tadpoles in muddy waters, scratched lines on her fingers from branches and weeded reeds that probably burned whenever they were washed with soap. She dug her fingers in the fruit with a splash, took the mulberries out in handfuls and filled them in buckets; in the mulberries, at the moment the fingers dug in, the hands listening to the chimes of the thousands of mulberry fruits, as if they had lodged themselves in the still pulsating body in order to love its soul; everything has stopped to see the only thing; it seems to you like you are the world, and now the whole world that is you is following through your eyes the movements of the hands digging in the fruit and equally filling up in handfuls the red, blue, green buckets and cups lined up on the ground; grandma's fingers make the mulberry even sweeter; you're all sitting on the dry-ish bench of the courtyard eating in silence, breaking off the barely holdable stems with cutters; enjoying bird calls, relishing blissfully; your soft, bony fingers duel in the bucket, all of them working on catching the big and ripe fruits; mixed in with the fruits are twigs from the tree marked with one or two sprouted young leaves; you constantly shake the bucket, because you all know that the tastiest and biggest fruits have a tendency to hide at the bottom; here you are, having reached your house with weightless steps, you are standing with a bloated belly on the threshold, proudly holding in your hand your family's share in a little bucket filled with mulberries; you knock on the door, there's no sound; you knock, they don't open, you wait, pressing your sweaty forehead against the door, then you sit on the doormat, which has just been sprinkled with water, you lean with your back against the door and put the bucket between your legs; you sing a song under your breath, your eyelids feel heavier, you body is tired from deep stress and emotion, your muscles are moaning, your eyes are closing, the sound of the fruits falling on the mulberry cloth, glglglglglglglglglgl the cloth sewn from shrouds and from the tree—the long-awaited fruits falling from the branches shaking like crazy—white, juicy, big and small, greenish, with hues appearing in dreams, like pouring rain, drops of sun fall from the sky, fall on your face, your head, your shoulders, the tip of your nose, they stroke your cheek, brush over your eyelashes, and fall into your lap; falling drop, now, from above, you only see the mouth of the boy's body buried under the mulberry fruits and only his smile, which gradually grows wider and wider, as it recalls the desire of the hands to hold one end of the cloth.

The dust film on the glass of the window made the trunk of the tree fade away, but after standing for a long time, his eyes penetrated through the denseness and he saw dark green here and there on the bark, imprints like glowing coal, wrinkles, protruding round twigs, with pared stiff sprigs sticking out, it was so different from all the natural and artificial pits, tiny insignificant grazes from randomly pointed fragments, examining the deep traces, which look like closed wounds with gray fillings, he was counting the insects crawling over the trunk of the tree, he knew by heart the open pores in the cracks. The bark was like drought-cracked ground. The sprinkled ashy hue on the whiteness of the snow is broken up into dark cracks in which darkness freezes. He would create images for himself, mixing the arrangement of wrinkles and turning them into portraits, he would contort his face, and with his pocket knife in front of the mirror he would slowly cut into his skin, peeling it, trying to resemble the trunk's hemlines. He didn't feel stinging pains. The streams of blood flowing from the cracks moved away from the neck and filled the earth. If his grandfather hit on the head of that long rusty crooked nail with his hammer now and the nail was driven into one of the cracks of his face, maybe he wouldn't feel any pain and he wouldn't be crying on his knees under the oleaster tree, because he was shocked and shaking from the surprise, which was like an unimaginable image. His mind hurt from the uncontrollable emotional outburst. The frosty-white little leaves of the oleaster fluttered from the shaking body on the ground, because the grandfather with whom every day he watered the trees in the orchard, dug under the trunks, painted the trunks white, weeded out the weeds, squeezed the brittle soil in their hands raised to the sun, the grandfather, who pruned the branches of the trees with a gentle but curt gaze while he walked behind him carefully collecting them, was suddenly at dawn angrily hitting hard with a hammer in his hand on the head of a rusty crooked nail on the trunk of the apple tree, driving it into the bark, deep, deep, whereas he had woken up from his sleep and had run barefoot to his grandfather and had frozen at the sight. Grandfather's hammer angrily rose and fell on the head of the nail, which disappeared into the trunk like a hopelessly foundering rowboat, it was as if the nail were driven into his body, piercing his skin, flesh, bone, piercing, piercing a lot, every strike that fell on the head of the nail shook his body; he had covered his ears with the palms of his hands, but the sound was already on its way in and he was no longer able to grasp whether the sound was coming from the outside or the inside; the brutal sound, which pulverized, with every strike, the garden of paradise, which had been created in the orchard, with his grandfather, among the trees, under the shade of their foliage and hanging fruits, for the trees, whose trunks he and his grandfather would embrace with both arms and put their heads against their warm and pulsating barks. It was his grandfather who had taught him to run to the orchard barefoot when he woke up in the morning and hug a tree, wrap himself around the trunk and stand still for a few minutes; the tree will love you, it'll give you what it has inside. And now his grandfather, who hugged the tree and put his head on the bark with him every morning, was driving the rusty nail into the tree, swearing under his breath and dispensing curses, and he ran, kneeled under the oleaster tree and cried, not listening to himself. In his mind, only the hammer that had descended on the head of the nail clanked, leaving the world without a single screech, and above his head, between the clouds, the sunset-colored clusters of oleaster trembled like church bells on quaking earth; his bare knees, which resembled axed young tree trunks sticking out of the earth, appeared through his tears, but the nail had already been driven to the end, the hammer had fallen on the fallen autumn leaves, because his grandfather had caught his sobs and had run under the oleaster tree, had hugged him, and kissing his cheeks had stroked his head with his rough hands and wiped his tears with his muddy fingers. His eyes burned from the mud filling up in his eyelids, but the sound of the hammer gradually faded and the strikes drowned in the distance, in some endless place; he had put his head on his grandfather's chest, but could not calm down, between the sobs, he tried to say something or other, his words flew out disconnected and fragmented; his grandfather had understood, he was calming him down, kissing him endlessly–on the head, the arms, the cheeks, the eyes, the neck. A tree won't grow fruit until it feels pain, don't worry, the nail won't hurt it, it'll help it, so that many, many, many clinking apples, sweet like you, apples with red cheeks are born, you got scared? don't be scared, the tree won't dry out, it'll feel a light prick and that's it, the prick of the nail will help it grow, all right, stop now, your face is lost in mud, let's go wash ourselves, stop now.

The wind and rain changed the colors of the tree trunk. From dawn to dusk, the mirror of the tree had become his window, the reflection of his pocked face. He wondered whether he would stay in the tree's memory or whether he would be irreversibly forgotten; the next soldier who will be here after him, when he looks out of the window, will he see his pallid face imprinted on the tree trunk, how many tree trunks are there in the world in front of hospital windows that are reproducing the last looks on people's faces? The tree is so quiet that it has no blood. You are so quiet that you have no blood, he whispered. Lying in bed, it was as if the tree were in him, he could feel the limited space of its dense weight. The light movements of his hands and legs made the tree tilt, pulling out its roots, and causing severe pains. The rush of the wind made the swishing of the leaves unbearable, he tried to hush them, but he couldn't see the branches, they were high up, very high up, where only the wind whooshed. He had started to feel sorry for himself, carefully in the beginning, afraid of that nasty little feeling that was unnoticeably nestling itself in his head; he felt sorry for his body, his thoughts, his clothes, then he felt sorry for the moment the guys amicably smiled at him and answered his questions, he felt sorry for the first time he entered Seda's room and took a bite of the darkness, the crumbling of the little flower in the flowerpot on his lap and the flow of the soil, he felt sorry for the girl's chuckle and ringing laughter, then he felt sorry for the scars on his skin left behind by the knife, he felt sorry for having had in his mouth the girl's only two canines, which glistened in the dark like the eyes of a little beast noticing a predator, one by one he felt sorry for all the twenty-something years he had lived, all the events and incidents, feelings, the going home after parties, the listening to Bob Dylan, of collecting all his records and dressing in his style, the moment he scored a goal, when the goalkeeper was running after the ball embarrassed, he felt sorry for the goalkeeper's embarrassment, he moved to taxi drivers, who looked for change for a thousand drams in different pockets of their pants and shirts and finding it, smiled, he felt sorry for voicing his Parisian wish, for all the scarves in the world, the tables and chairs of the city's cafés, the people who talked with each other, laughed and didn't think that they were going to die, he felt sorry for his thoughts that they were going to die, he felt sorry for the moment he bought his cigarettes from the newsstand, when he pointed out the pack he wanted to the saleswoman through the window, he felt sorry for the mangled cat in the middle of the street, for the footsteps of the man who put the cat in the box and walked out of the street, but most of all he felt sorry for his spreading of butter and jam on the crust of toasted bread, bringing it up to his mouth, chewing it, and sipping tea over it; he would even get out of bed with pantomimic gestures, trying to create similar images; first he would take a spoon, drive it into the butter, take it out, and spread it on the bread, then he would smear the orange jam on the butter, take a bite of the bread in his mouth and start to chew, then he would take the cup of tea and take a sip, and it was right at that moment that his level of shivers was pitiful, because he could see the inevitable perfection of loneliness, he could see it as obviously and clearly as the crust of bread, the jam, and the butter.

Some time later, after sobering up, he would somehow try to challenge or wipe out that ordinary experience running through his head, he would pull a pillow over his head and scream: done, done, done, I'm not coming out of this room, I'm not! The doctor had started to appear less, his voice was more likely to be heard, if you want, give me your home number, I'll call and let your family know, let them come and move you to another base. No, thanks, I don't want to move to another base, I won't leave my base. Fine, it's up to you, and doesn't your tooth hurt, can I pull it out, if, of course, you're not against it? No, I don't want it, go already, I'm fine. His voice was moving away. The blisters on his skin had scabbed, causing severe itchiness. He would get out of his room at night, run down the narrow hospital hallway screaming, banging his back, his shoulders, his forehead against the walls, he wanted to scratch, to completely take off his stinging, burning skin, if only to stop the itching, to calm down, even for just one minute, and sleep. It had been three days already that no food had been brought from the mess hall. They're staying away, he thought, they don't want to touch my plate, my spoon, my fork, or greet me with a handshake; touch my skin with their fingers, breathe my air, stand next to me, hear my voice, see my room, my thermometer, everything planned with my life. Shadows appeared in the hallway of the hospital, from the half-open door of the room, you could see contorting, distorted objects. Water filled inside from the cracks in the floor. As he ran through the puddles of water formed in the hallway, his shadow imprinted itself on walls moment after moment and the water's firework-like spatters froze in the air. He was shredding pages from the Bible and Narek, crumpling them, stuffing them in his mouth, mincing them with his teeth, spitting them out, it's hailing, hailing, my brother, he was screaming, I'm making hail out of the pages, tooltaltitooltaltilmatiltal. It had started to rain in the room. He was tensely examining the ceiling, besides the flaky plaster that somehow hung onto the walls, there were no holes. From what he remembered, the roof of the hospital was strong, of metal, but who knew from where the heavy rain was gradually flooding the room. He pulled the blanket over his head, trying to protect himself. The wetness had made the blanket so heavy that it seemed as if his body under the weight, wherever it was, would explode like a pumpkin. A layer of cold water had covered the blanket. He was lying on the water, but he couldn't feel the water, only the coldness of the white bed cover. People appeared in the hallway, he could hear footsteps, he would call out to them, no one responded, they approached one by one, looked at him through the open crack of the door of his room, and left. They were unfamiliar eyes. Maybe new soldiers were being admitted to the hospital or the doctor had finally found his home number and had told his mother about his condition. Mom, he screamed, did you come? I'm here, come in! The whispers behind the door stopped. Little children also gathered by the door, you could hear the sound of their crawls and see their soft little hands through the door. Hold the children, whose children are they? Please help them, they're going to drown, they'll swallow water, children have small lungs, pick them up. He constantly called out, cried, doctoooor, guuuuys, come in, I'm not sleeping. He thought that the task force of the mess hall had felt sorry for him and sent him food, or that the guys of the company had talked to Cardinal, had come to an agreement, had forgiven him, and had come to the hospital to visit him. Everybody was silent. He understood that his sickness retreated by the hour and brought him closer to a fateful return. Sometime next week, the doctor will probably discharge me, the guys will be waiting for me right by the entrance, he would repeat to himself, shrinking under the concrete blanket. When he opened up his eyes in the morning, he was at sea, lying in a flat rowboat. All around him was boundless water with rippling turquoise waves. Suddenly, from looking at the water for a long time, heads of people and children appeared in the waves that were watching him with gaping, unblinking eyes. The light oscillation of the ripples made their heads bob like buoys, but no one turned their gaze another way, all of them were staring at him, suddenly bringing their faces right up to his. He screamed with all the strength he had left inside of him: doctor! Only the sound of splashes could be heard. He screamed again, jumped out of bed into the water, and swam forwards like a lunatic. His arms had gotten tired with cold and weakness. It seemed to him that he was still lying in bed, that he was merely flapping his arms weakly in the air, sinking them into the water without getting wet. He didn't find the door of the room, he stopped swimming and only moved his legs in order not to drown. He suddenly felt something sticky press against the back of his neck, he quickly turned around: it was a kitten with a deformed head and a thin red stream with white spots pouring out of its mouth. He closed his eyes. The little kitten had probably been thrown under the boat, the prow of the boat had hit its head and killed it; if there were a box, I'd take it and bury it somewhere, the poor young of a cat in the waves, stay well. There was no point in swimming forwards, he could feel himself losing his strength, he swam back, somehow reached the rowboat, lay down, and fell into a deep sleep. A pleasant morning wind was blowing. Above his head, jays had appeared circling around the rowboat. He fumbled all the pockets of his pants. He pulled out random things, faded wall paper, medicine; he angrily threw all of it in the water. Suddenly he felt a tap on his shoulder, he turned around and saw his soldier's hat, he picked it up and started fumbling its lining, he found and pulled out a hidden pin. Getting his breath back in order, he made himself comfortable; he held his breath once more, then exhaling quiveringly he took off his shirt and, with the tip of the pin, he began to poke all of the blisters on his chest and belly, in the beginning slowly, carefully, coming to terms with the pain, then frantically, he pierced the blisters, digging as deep as possible, moving on to this arms, legs, shoulders, face. The pain had intensified so much that he couldn't feel, on the contrary, he was enveloped by some sort of freedom that numbed his body and felt like it was pushed between vertical ice cubes. He felt a light weight on his knee, he vigilantly peeled his eyes and saw a naked girl with familiar eyes, thin, practically the size of a matchbox, who was holding the flower in the flowerpot that was on the window sill of the patient room, and she now looked at him sadly, now at the movements of the pin. Sed? Is that you? Hi. Happiness made him come to for a moment, he wanted to hold the girl in his arms, but couldn't, she was so small he was afraid to hurt her; he gently stroked her shoulder. Then he saw how the girl opened up the palm of her hand in which there was a 10 cc syringe, how she put the flower in her arms into the syringe, carefully pushing the tip of the needle into the vein of her arm that had fallen on the edge of his knee and injecting it to the end, and now that she was sitting with sort of naive eyes, a naive tilt of the neck, either with muscles or muscular, but sweet, mild-tasting, because it was a girl's naive little eyes, she, too, couldn't figure out how she had loved and gone to say I love you and bring him the flower in the flowerpot in his room as a gift, well, who knows, she thought that the head of the flower, the green stalk, the red petals, the clay would made him happy; he liked all of her body's curves and arrows left on her skin cut by prickly beards that will fade away when you die from some disease, or you'll get run over by a car, or someone will shoot you in the throat, the grass roots under the earth will feed off your scars, yeah, those lines, do they hurt, I wonder, or burn? the body was created a long time ago, when the world was deprived of memory, and he could not understand why he was lying in the room with plain, memorable furniture, in the dark room, as a body taller than the piles of clothes strewn on the floor, your children will probably live here later, they will play with the twirling dark shadows instead of the piles, forgetting the little teddy bear and the flowers dressed in colorful outfits, and the cars with naked skeletons; unopened bed, your body unopened, ungiven, it was closed and someone who did not feel closeness inside of you was moaning, did not remember that he hasn't been born yet and that unborn he is waiting for you; the line that stretches from your neck to your shoulder is the distance of my pleasure, my desire to live, my descent to slide down from, I'll make myself comfortable somewhere between the bodies, in one of the grooves of your lips, in your little philtrum dimple, I'll close my ears and I'll put my ear to your heart—thump-thump-thump—then every day the same room, the same blanket, the same bed sheet, pillow, bed, everything; you've changed your skin a few times, so what, the sheets being clean or dirty has nothing to do with your birth, and the flower in the clay flowerpot on the window sill that was a peculiar, unnecessary beauty with red petals from which every morning your heart filled with incomprehensible and meaningless rapture; the flower was small, its bud the size of an iris, the soil of the flowerpot with unsealable cracks was moist. He decided to visit Seda on the eve of his leaving to the army and confess his love to her. He decided to offer her the flower in the clay flowerpot on the window sill in his room. That day he had, according to himself, worn his best clothes, but in front of the mirror his shirt looked somehow big, as if it were a blown-up bag drooping from his missing shoulders. He would continuously see a dot on his collar, but whenever he took it off and minutely examined it, the dot would disappear. He combed his hair, now to the right, now to the left, he parted it on the side, then groomed it all forward and tilting his head he examined that look that was in no way taking shape. It was not attractive, it's as if he were a young man having just graduated from school with flawed facial features. He looked for happiness in his eyes, but saw expectation and courage. His eyes welled up with a soft fear and were defeated by a long stare. He practically washed himself with perfume. He sprayed from the phial a few times, then ran back and forth, cutting the scattered and gradually vanishing droplets of dust cubes in the air. Then he looked attentively in the mirror, as if he were trying to see the fragrance of the perfume exuding from his clothes. Holding the flowerpot in his arms, he left the house, stopped the first taxi he saw in the street and went to Seda's house. The street where the girl lived had turns like a snake and was full of homeless packs of dogs. He remembered the first time his brother took him to Seda, and then, as they got out of the house in a great mood, the first delight of his life was ruined by those same dogs, which snarled at first and, showing the sparkle of their sharp fangs, surrounded them and went mad, forcing them to run away terrified, falling and getting up, until one of the elderly men living on that street, cursing and shaking the stick in his hand in the air, scared them and made them flee. At that time there were four of them, him, his brother, and two of his brother's friends. He was the last to enter Seda's room, and until that moment he was sitting in the living-room touching the skin of his neck with his fingers. He stood naked in the dark and wouldn't move forward. The air in the room was heavy with emotional feeling. In front of him, the head of the bed was sketched out. For a moment he thought that maybe the girl was the shadow that had embraced his body and shackled his movements, maybe she was now stroking and kissing him. He stuck his hand out, sunk deep into the denseness, then he opened his mouth and took a bite of the darkness. The tips of his fingers touched the girl's fingers. Come here, he heard a hoarse and tired voice. He walked, trampling a pile of clothes strewn on the floor. The girl embraced his thigh with her arm. He trembled, slowly gliding his gaze down, his half-twisted feet open wide, it was a thin swaying layer of snow, from which a soft wind blew. Your brother told me that I'm going to be your first. He tried to pick out a hint of irony or mockery, it was all kindness. He tried to remember her uttered words a second time, but he didn't get to; the girl took him by the arm and gently pulled him towards her. He lay down on the thin layer of snow and softly put his head on the girl's shoulder. Seda dug her fingers in his hair and started to caress the back of his neck. The girl kissed his shoulder, the tip of her tongue through her lips touched his skin. You've never been loved with a tongue? The girl's question sounded so ordinary that it seemed as if the question had no expectation whatsoever of hearing an answer. Then they changed position, and that he felt, when the girl's tongue playing naughtily began to dance freely over his body. He closed his eyes and with his hand he began to stroke her sporadically shaking head. Then he felt a strange sensation, as if the whole world submersed at a slow, very slowly pace, in a light with palpable walls. He understood that their bodies' gradually accelerating sweetness of rhythm, second after second, turned the last morsels of consciousness into dust. The light engulfed his body, and his body's final feeling of loss and forgetting gave him a perfect happiness that he had never felt in his life. Then, when he was already home, he thought about that moment when he put his head on her shoulder, the thin layer of snow, and the circling tongue and light over his body. In the light of his memory, he in no way felt the presence of his brother and his two friends.

He took Seda's phone number and began to visit her twice a week. He'd call and they would agree on a day, time, and price. Seda taught him how to make love with her frail body; she taught him not to hurry, to kiss deeply, trusting the swaying rhythms of the tongue and body. In the beginning they only had sex in the dark, which concealed his insecurity. Every quick movement, every redundancy was smoothed out by the sharp sensitivity of Seda's experienced body. But the girl got him used to daylight nudity and making love with open eyes, without sheets or covers. When he touched Seda's body in the dark, he only felt his touch and imagined the body, but in the daylight he saw his touch and watched her body. His imagination of the girl's body was more accessible in the dark than in the day-light, in which the clear visibility of her skin, bones, and facial expressions intractably repelled him, causing sweet pain to his mind and multiplying his desire to finish. When he stroked her breast and saw the strokes, it thrilled him, because the moment of his hand touching her breast seemed unlikely and it seemed unlikely when he saw the affection of their tongues and their open eyes staring steadfastly at their tongues. Seeing his touch-ing the girl's body meant seeing the unlikely. He gently rubbed his lips, he felt the lines of scars with pink streaks in areas on her belly and breasts, the hardened fluid inside the scars, which were leftover traces of cuts of knives and razors, and he very much wanted, simply dreamed, that all of his touches, all of his thrills and kisses would be exceptional in the girl's memory. He had learned to kiss the girl so warmly and gently that Seda closed her eyes and fell into sweet shivers. No one kisses me like you, the girl barely whispered with her eyes closed. Seda gave him discounts, if at a particular moment, he didn't have enough money, she slept with him for free. Seda only had two sharp canines in her mouth that were white and glistening, her lips were like the yellowish line of a page ripped apart and glued together again. She was short, thin, and small boned. In the feeble light, for a moment she looked like an old grandmother whose bones replaced rippling grass under her skin. Her facial features were worn like the edges of a table. She lived with her bedridden mother and generally invited clients to her house and to the same room. When he slept with Seda, he thought about the light with palpable walls, and when he slept alone, he also thought about the light with palpable walls. He asked the girl to lightly sink her two canines into his back and slide down with them. When Seda laughed, opening her mouth wide and displaying her canines, he understood that besides those two lonely sharp-edged teeth, she had nothing else of worth in her life. And he was convinced that if Seda ever lost her canines, her life would end. The light gradually seized all the shadowy areas; his existence now was planned by the light. It was the light that became his only contact, illusion, and reality. And he no longer went to the light, because he lived inside the light.

The taxi stopped in front of Seda's own house. Holding the flower in the flowerpot in his arms, he knocked twice on the door of the gate. Sounds of an intense conversation trickled out from the inside. The door was opened by a guy with a black blouse and shriveled-up wrestler's ears. Who do you want? I've come to see Seda. The guy in the black blouse stared at the flowerpot in his arms. Do you have an appointment? Yeah, I have an appointment. The guy opened the door wide and let him in. They walked for a long time through the garden to the spiral staircase. Seda's room was on the second floor. The noise of laughter and swearing from above intensified. The guy with the shriveled-up ears practically ran up the stairs and disappeared from view. He hesitated for a moment and then also began to climb up, brushing the metal balusters of the staircase, which were dusty and pleasant, with the palm of his hand. Putting his shoulder against the door of the living room, he pushed and went in. His eyes squinted from the smoke and stench. About twenty people were sitting around the living-room table playing cards, smoking, and drinking. Everyone turned to him. Good day to you. It was as if the smoke was so dense that it choked his voice. Hello, hello came from the table. I've come to see Seda. Good for you, my brother, we've also come to see Seda, come on in. Laughter exploded. It was as if his legs were missing; he had frozen, but he recognized the hand that was holding the flower in the flowerpot. Give the guy a chair, let him sit. One of the guys brought him chair, but he only saw his fingers lost in dirt. He moved the chair as close as possible to the only door that opened from Seda's room to the living-room and slowly sat down, not putting down the flower in the flowerpot in his arms. The guys were of middle age with thick stubbles and dark clothes. Their shoes with worn noses were visible under the table. A sharp smell of sweat and *oghi*[11] wafted from them, and whenever they laughed, a row of gold teeth in their mouth glistened. They played with spastic movements, constantly spitting on the floor and cussing each other out. The door of Seda's room opened. He jumped out of the chair, thinking it was the girl. It was a tall, lanky guy drenched in sweat, without a shirt, his belt undone.

Niiiiiiiiiiiiiiiiiiiiiiiiiiiiiiiiiiiiiiiice, someone bawled from the table. Thanks, my brother, hope you get the same, pour a glass, let's drink. With half-closed eyes, drops of sweat frozen on his forehead, licking his lips, the guy hiccupped with short intervals and rubbed his hairy stomach. It's my turn, I'm going. Throwing the playing cards in front of him, a guy barely got up from one corner of the table and started to undress, taking off

---

11   Popular Armenian vodka-like spirit distilled with fruits and berries.

his shirt, his undershirt in the beginning, then he undid his belt, his coffin-like shoes, his pants, he put his shoes back on, and with the bounds of a rabbit he kicked the door of Seda's room, went in, and slammed the door shut behind him. They split into new pairs and, keeping the score on a pack of cigarettes with a pen, continued to play. Now and then the game was interrupted either with some mindless argument or with fresh toasts. After drinking the *oghi*, they would all take turns biting from the *matnakash*[12] bread and passing it on to the next person. Brother, will you drink a glass with us? Pour the guy a drink; bring over your chair. He left the chair in its place, without putting the flower in the flowerpot down from his arms, he quietly got up, approached the table, took the glass that was poured for him, then went back and sat by the door to Seda's room. A few of them sitting at the table cast glances at him full of anger and disgust. Was your back hurting, my brother, or you just couldn't be bothered to clink our glasses? He quietly got up again with the flowerpot, approached the table, and extended his glass. The clinks of glasses could be heard. Everyone's mouth was agape. Without saying a word, he downed the drink, put the glass on the table, and went to sit in his chair. He looked at the flowerpot attentively: the cracks were deep; it was as if there were a bottomless pit inside, he himself considered the flower watered when water flooded out of the cracks with a belch. But very often it seemed as if the cracks were so deep that even a few tons of water wouldn't be enough to fill them. The little flower was in the middle of the soil, right on the edge of one of the dark cracks. The curly root of the flower, thinner than a sprout, had come out of the soil and bridged the crack.

---

12   Type of bread typical to Armenia. It resembles *barbari* bread.

It seemed to him that if he made one erratic move, the flower would fall in the crack and die; he anxiously pressed the flowerpot even harder against his chest. The door of the room opened. Completely naked, with dark-red cheeks, the guy came out, stood in the middle of the living room and screamed, ooooooooooaaaaaaaah, what was this, my God, she killed, yanked, fifteen minutes and boom! "Put your clothes on, you dumbass!" came from the table. A ball of crumb was thrown at him. Give me something to smoke, let me catch my breath. Someone took a cigarette out of a pack, put it between his lips, and lit it with a lighter. With a cigarette in his mouth, barely able to keep his balance, he began to get dressed. He saw on the guy's wet shoulder, a little apart from each other, two pink scratches. He squinted a few times and his jaw quivered. I'm gooooooooooing, it's my tuuuuuuuurn. The guy with the short-shaved haircut got up so fast and went into Seda's room that everyone raised their finger in amazement. His mother looked after the flower; his mother looked after it and he enjoyed its beauty. His mother liked to look after the flower more than looking at it, while his eyes opened in the morning for the flower, and he was convinced that the flower, every morning, examined him with the same amount of interest. His mother never poured cold water in the flowerpot. When the weather got warm, she took the flower to the balcony, and put the flowerpot in a gentle ray of sun. One time the flower had weakened. It's getting sick, he said, mom, and holding the flower in his arms, he went to the doctor. The doctor prescribed medicine, they were orange-like pills with white dots, every day, at dawn, when he was still in bed, with a rolling pin in her hand, his mother would enter his room, crush the pill, sprinkle it under the flower, and pour water over it. The flower stretched towards the light again. The door of the room opened and closed. The guy with the shaved head sashayed into the living room and approached the table, took a bite from the *matnakash* and started to chew with relish, mumbling disgruntled under his breath, she's exhausted, she doesn't moan, doesn't make a sound, doesn't feel anything, I scratched her skin with a knife, still didn't mean anything to her, she doesn't feel anything, she's really dead, who have you brought me to? He approached the table almost with tears in his eyes, sat in a chair, lit a cigarette, and started to nervously take one quick puff of smoke after another, tapping undeveloped ash into the ashtray every few seconds. Everyone started messing with him. They lightly slapped him on the nape, the cheeks, they kicked the tips of the noses of his shoes. Aaaaah, you couldn't do anything and you blame the whore, from someone who does it right, they feel every single thing, here, look at what your brother will do. The door of Seda's room opened and closed. Suddenly he saw her from the table; he was sitting, holding the flowerpot with the flower tightly in his arms, with an uncertain gaze. Around the hand that held the flowerpot, on the surface of the clay, traces of moisture could be noticed. They had been formed by the sweaty palm of his hand. He felt anxious, maybe the moisture would harm the flowerpot and it would start to crack before he could give it to Seda. But a little later he calmed down, remembering that baked clay was hard. The door of the room opened and closed again. The next guy had already undressed a long time ago and was impatiently waiting for his turn. He was pacing around the living room, smoking, and cursing the police officers who had stopped his car a few months earlier and written out a heavy fine. After throwing a few hysterical jokes his way, his friends focused on the card game, forgetting his presence. In turn, the naked body of the waiting guy now disappeared in the thick layer of smoke that enveloped the room, now appeared in the suspended little cloud. It was as if he were an unfortunate and mysterious ghost, tormented in his own solitude. When he entered Seda's room, he took with his body a giant cloud of smoke. At the Chinese restaurant, Seda bit the fried bread and extended it to him, she showed the two little marks left by her sharp canines, and he leaned over and kissed the girl's glistening oily lips, they were laughing so loudly that the waiter complained to the manager. They were told something about it, which made their laughter gather renewed strength. Seda once confessed that his body was a carbon copy of his brother's body, everything was the same, even his movements and the smell of his skin, everything grew dark before his eyes, he grabbed her throat, he wanted to choke her, he had lost his mind with anger, his hands were shaking, and Seda was laughing and sticking her tongue out between her canines, but noticing his strong reaction, she apologized and said that she was joking, that she didn't remember the moment she had sex with his brother, and in general hasn't remembered a single body, movement, or skin smell in a long time, because she doesn't feel, except for his kisses—warm, soft, and deep—she swore, she feels, believe it. At night that day, under his covers, he cried a lot and, in general, ever since he had gotten to know the girl, he cried a lot, but quietly, without feelings. The surprise tears suddenly streamed down his cheeks, wetting his lips and sheets. He had even started to cry in his dreams, he'd wake up with a completely wet face, he'd turn to his side and, stretching out his fingers, he'd caress the dark and bite it, opening and closing his mouth. The door of the room opened. The guy came out with a satisfied look on his face, he lit a cigarette and lay down smack in the middle of the living room, his gaze turned to the flowerpot. Eh, brother, by the time your turn comes, only the stalk will be left. Letting out puffs of smoke, he dissipated them with his hand, tapping the ash into his navel, then he got up, said that it was the first time he noticed his nudity, ran to his clothes scattered by the table and quickly began to dress. The door of Seda's room opened and closed with a bang. Brother! My brother! Hellooooooooooooooooooooo, oooooooooooo-ooooooooooo. He looked indifferently at the table. My brother, can I ask something, how much do you pay Seda, if it's not a secret, eh, just out of interest? He was quiet for a long time, then, without opening his mouth, he uttered, I don't pay. The conversations around the table died. What, are you serious? Guys, did you hear that? This slut gets fucked for free! Oh, man, no, are you serious? You don't give her money and she agrees? Oh, maaaaaan, and she wants 5000 drams one by one from each of us, yeaaaah, OK, OK, OK, so this is what we'll do, just wait, when Zar comes out, four of us will go in and we'll show her what we've got, no one should cheat us, wait, you watch what we do to her. His heart started pounding fast, he felt stings around his throat. No, no, I also pay, it's just that one time she didn't take anything, just one time, but I paid her later, it's just that at that moment I didn't have enough on me, that's why she didn't take anything, otherwise I've always paid, I always pay, guys, please, you don't need to do anything! The door of the room opened again. They filled the glasses with *oghi* and, flapping around, knocked them back to the end. Well, as I said, four of us are going in now, let's go. Four guys got up, took their shirts off, untied their belts, and went into the room single file, one after another. The girl's hoarse squeals were heard from the room for the first time. The smack of a hard slap suddenly resounded. The guys sitting by the table started cackling. Seda's shriek sounded sharper the second time and it was again cut short with a heavy slap. He jumped up, pushed the door with his foot, and went into the girl's room. Seda was buried completely naked under the bodies of four broad-shouldered guys who were beating her with their hands and feet. Leave Seda alone, what are you doing? Lea… the word was cut off, because he felt a sharp pain on the back of his neck that cut his breath. Not dropping the flower with the flowerpot, he fell on the naked bodies. Dropping ruthless strikes on him, they dragged him to the middle of the living-room and twenty people continued to beat him. His departing consciousness threw a fork very close to his fingers. He groped for the fork and stabbed someone's groin. Then the clay flowerpot shattered and the soil poured into his arms. He felt a wet bliss inside of him. He tried to find the flower with one glance of the eye, but he could no longer see, his eyes had been shut closed by two big blood swellings formed from the beatings. The flower probably fell into my arms with the soil, he calmed himself down a little and understood that he was lying on Seda's lost-in-blood and cut-up skin, because he suddenly felt the familiar melting of a thin layer of snow; he smiled and gently put his head on the girl's shoulder, as if he were protecting and embalming her life with his shroud. The light gradually swallowed up his whole body and his body's final feeling of loss and forgetfulness once more gave him perfect happiness, which he felt on that day when he entered Seda's room for the first time.

He couldn't take the morning pain anymore, he had fallen to the floor, he was screaming, clenching the foot of the bed with his teeth, bubbly foam streaming out of his mouth. The blisters pounded like a heart and he listened to the beats of all of them one by one, each one differing in speed and pain. The door of the room opened, he turned his head indifferently and he saw a soldier through the brown cloud. Mickey Mouse was standing in the room with a dinner tray in his hand. He shuddered, for a moment it seemed as if his teeth moved to the foot of the bed and gnashed together. He somehow managed to lean on his knees; he closed his eyes and opened them again; it was Mickey. He had brought food: soup, boiled wheat, tea, bread, butter and jam. Mickey's hands and sensitive lips trembled; he wasn't saying anything. You've brought food, huh? Me, you brought me food, son of a bitch? He screamed in pain and struck his knee with his fist. Mouse put the tray on the floor and, cowering, tried to approach him; noticing Mickey's footsteps, he jumped up terrified, stood on his bed, and started to run side to side like a madman. Stay where you are, Mick. Stay where you are. Don't come here. Don't come close. Stay where you are, I'm telling you, stay! Don't move; don't move again; don't touch anything. Stay, I'm telling you. I'll kill you, don't come forward; stay. Confused, Mick took a few steps back and hit the door with his back. He put his head under the covers, but through a narrow crack he could see Mickey Mouse, who was growing thinner and thinner with every passing moment. Come here. Come here. Don't touch the door. Mick. Don't touch the door. Piece of shit, filthy animal. Don't touch the door. You touched it? Your back touched the door? Tell me! I'm sorry, with my shoulder. I lightly tapped it with my shoulder. Mickey hung his head. He tried to climb up the needles of the spruce that had grown in the distant corner, but his muscles were frail and powerless. Your shoulder tapped against it. How did you do it? How did it tap against it? Come here, Mick. I'm saying, come here. But don't come close to me. Don't. Show me your hands. With his eyes peeled to the floor, Mick extended his hands. You're not wearing gloves? Why aren't you wearing gloves? Where are your gloves? I have them on, I'm wearing them, you don't see them, I'm wearing them, Mick replied, barely able to hold back his tears. He crouched down, picked up the tray from the floor, the moist in his eyes blocked his visual field. You need to be moved to a state hospital, you're not well, Mickey's feeble voice echoed. Shhhhhhhhhhhhhh-hhhhh, Mickey, shhhhhhhhhhhh, shut up, if you tell anyone about this, I'll cut your throat, you hear? You didn't see me, tell whoever sent you that the door of my room was locked with a key, understood? Swear you won't tell the guys, do that one thing, swear, you hear? We didn't see each other, mouse. If you want, I'll only tell the doctor, so he can help you. No, no, no, noooooooooooooo, no, no, I told you, aren't you listen to what I'm telling you? You didn't see me, period, you want me to get out of here and kill you, huh? At least eat a bit of bread. Mickey's lower lip had turned white and was twitching. Go, Mick, like a brother, go, please, go. Don't think about the bathroom, I'll clean it for the both of us. He didn't let Mick continue, he flew out like a ball, kicked the edge of the tray with his foot, knocked it all over Mickey, darted back again, and huddled in a corner of the bed. The hot soup drenched Mickey's field shirt, the tray and tableware collapsed on the floor. Mickey stood frozen for a long time with uncertainty. Then he slowly moved his finger to his cheek, wiped the piece of butter, crouched down, and one by one picked up the tray, collected the tableware, and, casting a glance in his direction for the last time, he waddled off. He counted all of Mickey's footsteps in his head. The door of the hospital closed. In his dream he heard the sound of Mickey's footsteps, which were neither going nor coming. The next day he was barely able to move his left foot. Infections had become well-manifested around the bleeding blisters, with wounds here and there. With his very last bit of strength, he got out of the bed, crawled over the floor, pushed the door, went out into the hallway, and found the doctor's room with difficulty. It was strange: for some reason, the door was open, but there was no one inside. Dragging his body, he leaned with his back on the opposite side of the desk and fell asleep. It was getting light when he woke up. He opened the door of the cabinet, found a 10 cc syringe, took it, and returned to his room in the same condition, stretched himself out on the bed, made his back comfortable against the pillow, and took off his shredded and bloody shirt. From under the artificial shrub in the doctor's room, he had taken a handful of soil, which he started to sprinkle with care over the blisters and rubbing it in with his hand, as if he were grinding meat, then he opened the syringe, pulled out the plunger, gathered up a ball of saliva, and filled it up. With open eyes and holding his breath, he inserted the tip of the needle one by one under the blisters and injected; during the fifth injection, he lost consciousness, and when he opened his eyes, he didn't see anything other than the trunk of the tree. It was raining; he opened his eyes again, and when he awoke, he was standing with a suitcase in his hand going down the metro's escalator. All the way down, standing with a bunch of flowers in his hand, was Luke-Vacho, they embraced, Luke-Vacho took the suitcase out of his hand, gave him the bunch of flowers, he was asking him how his trip was, but he was in no mood, he was constantly scratching his armpit with his beak, moving around restlessly. So, your dream came true. Yeah, I totally am really in a dream, I can't believe I'm in Paris, I miss my brother like crazy, I imagine how happy he'll be. Luke-Vacho was sadly looking at the Seine's mouse-colored water. He won't be happy anymore. How? Why? Because he'll be forced to go home again. But I came, why home? You didn't come. You said goodbye. Who did I say goodbye to? Are you crazy, Luke-Vacho? What happened to you? Are you okay? We're stuck in the rain, let's run fast. It's not raining: they're holding the morgue's cold showerhead against your body.

When the doctor opened the door of the room of the soldier sick with chickenpox, his eyes twitched. Completely naked, the guy had wrapped himself around the foot of the bed like a fetus. Even the medical specialist shuddered when he saw him. It was impossible to count with any precision the number of marks left on his body by the needle. The guy had not taken care of a single part of his young body. There were a couple of 10 cc syringes in different corners of the room. His body was stiff like iron. Baffled, the medical specialist had turned around and was standing in front of the window, looking through the bars for a long time at the tree trunk. They started to work when the inspector arrived. Meticulously examining the soldier's torn body, the medical specialist noticed that there was something in his right hand; he tried to open his fist, but couldn't. Exerting great effort with his entire physical strength, he broke the guy's index finger and thumb and pulled back his axed fingers; in his hand was a comb.

two

There was so much noise in my life, Zizu thought and walked down the path, which was merely an unbroken little line, a silence that stretched in the grass. "Landmines in forest," the writing with thick careless letters on a piece of tin stayed behind and he began to run through the thick grass, which was warm and soft like a fur coat. The soldiers' voices gradually died away. He was running and looking back, terrified that the shadow running after him like a helpless puppy would catch up with him, fall under his feet, and throw down his body. Panting, he conquered the prickly hillock, stood at the top, put his hand on his burning chest, and looked. Below, a spruce, magnificent and sad, sprawled in the open space. He stood for a long time. He caught his breath and anxiously turned his ear to the distantly fading echo of his run. He couldn't hear anything. A narrow path vanished towards the spruce. He's waiting there, he's arrived, I know, he'll come. He went into the shade with his eyes closed, feeling with every step the mysterious touches against his body. In front of the infinitude of spruces outlined in the dark where the dense grass waves in the gentle breeze, he sees the course of his feeble feet and hears the rustle of the ripples of shaking blades of grass under the tremble of his feet. It seemed as if his body split in two in front of the path that was ribboned by a double row of spruces; one half froze in the ripple of the grass, its gaze fixed in fear at the vanishing shadows of the path, while the other half walked, closing its eye; he walked over that practically uncrossable path, giving himself to the unknown and to fate. The shadows of the trees swayed over the tiny little leaves and spruce needles under his feet, intensifying their colors. The peculiar sounds that could be heard in the deep silence suddenly stopped and resumed at short intervals, as if they were talking to each other, ignoring the silence. Those sounds were already different from those his ears were accustomed to: in them, there was the absence of man. Under his feet, the dry leaves crackled, the twigs snapped, suddenly a bird twittered, a spring purled from the depths of the lost hillock, the faint echo of a rolling rock could be heard in the distance, and sometimes the wave of a weak moan also struck. He would stop in his tracks, hold his breath, it would seem as if they were calling for help, he would sit on a mossy rock, focus with all of his senses, and wait for a long time. But as soon as he would sit down, the sounds disappeared. It was as if the forest fell silent with his waiting. And when he got up and walked, that peculiar moan was audible again. The forest, he thought, probably stored every single sound, whisper, shadow, and light in its memory; the footsteps, which are stamped into the grass, never vanish, and not a single soldier is ever forgotten after leaving his shadow to the soul of the forest. The memory of the forest is sound. The sky invisibly united the split tops of the spruces, closing the disk of the sun, the thin translucent rays through the foliage made their way into his body, came out, and entered the soil. He felt the flowing warmth of those rays passing through his body. On the way, here and there, the trees totally blocked all of the possible paths of light, burying the space in darkness. That darkness with a dark-greenish hue stroked the leaves, slowly streamed over his face, but it did not stop its course, on the contrary, it communicated some sort of weightless freedom to his steps. The darkness smelled of tree. But then suddenly one unexpected sharp ray of light tore up the black veil and, gliding down his shoulder, poured out in the grass. Mist revolved in the light. The silhouettes darkened, thickening the mist, then progressively opened up while moving, and dust particles that bore a resemblance to snowflakes became transparent and visible, swaying irregularly in the vertical opening. That ray of light was a narrow door, just like this path ribboned by a double row of spruces, he thought that it opened to the road that leads to the sun and that the sun was a door. On the way, whenever he came across dandelions crushed by the hooves of goats, he squinted, he would move forward, but the farther he moved from the broken stems of dandelions lying in the mud, the more he grew angry at the goats, their careless steps, the irresponsibility of the hooves, the defencelessness of the dandelions, not because they killed the flowers by breaking them, but because they crushed them, embalmed them with mud, and deprived them of their final hope to see the sun.

Not much had passed since the photograph of his beloved girl had fallen from his arms into the boat-like basin, since he had run like a madman and practically broken down the door of Mickey's woodshed. It was dawn, no one saw how Zizu and the little mouse approached the washbasin, how Mick took off one of his gloves and took out from under the soapy water and shaving foam his beloved girl sadly lying there, how he quickly shoved it down his chest and walked away, while he, in despair and furious at his own carelessness, went into the woodshed, threw his beret to the ground, and started to smash everything that fell into his hands until a splinter that flew off a wooden chair cut his arm and he began to cry, covering his face with both hands, because what had fallen in the washbasin was now forever lost. That night, Zizu quietly went to Mickey and asked him to dry the photograph as well as he could, and threatened him, saying that if he told anyone about the incident, he would definitely kill him. He went back the following night. Mickey had found an iron from who knows where and had dried the photograph by pressing it with the heat of the iron, and then, to prevent wear, he had glued the photograph to a piece of thick cardboard, even though he had not been able to fully remove the yellow stain and sporadic air bubbles. Every night he went to Mickey to look at his beloved girl's face for a half an hour. With his gloves, Mickey would hand over the photograph to him under a candlelight and close his eyes. But soon the light of the candle seemed too bright to him, and from fear of being discovered, his muscles would freeze in the morning, his fingers would stiffen like iron rods, he would separate from the guys and somehow hide his state of mind. He had written a letter to his girlfriend to get a new photograph, but he didn't know when it would arrive. In the evenings, he would go to bed with his clothes on. As soon as the night grew dark, when his numbness got worse, he quickly got out of bed, got out of the barracks, and ran to Mickey. Instead of candlelight, Mickey had started to exhibit the photograph under the flame of a lighter. He would hold the girl's photograph in front of his eyes with one hand and with the other he would light the lighter until the metal cap turned red with heat, then a three-minute break and again. He would take food to Mickey that he hidden under his shirt: boiled chicken leg, eggs, fried potato stuffed in bread, and chocolate. And when, on the last day, he found out that the commander of the battalion had assigned Mickey Mouse to the "Butterfly" front with the other soldiers to dig a trench, suddenly without warning and without thinking of the consequences, he ran to the backyard of the mess hall and found the guy leaning against the wall eating boiled lentils. He only managed to convey to Mickey that their bases were three kilometers apart, and that if he did not show up in three days, at his appointed time, in his given place—by the tree in the open field on the other side of the forest, which was an area full of mines—and didn't bring his girlfriend's photograph, he might as well consider himself dead. The last word came out jumbled. Water shadows squirted out of Zizu's eyes, he curtly turned around, wiped his eyes with his sleeve, and walked away. Without raising his head, Mickey went on eating the lentils with relish.

The forest unexpectedly cut into a big field, a sea of undulating grass. The light-green mystifying hue made him gasp. With criss-cross punches, the wind made the grass whistle, turning it darker, changing the color of the green, which grew thicker when it lay down and gleamed yellow when the wind penetrated through the verdure and infinitely rushed by. The grass was so free, so inviting and alone, and he was gliding through the freedom as if it were a tiny bit of eternity melting on the border of the area with rippling grass, and the wavering wind playing with his lips was so pleasant, when the grass swayed, it was so different, whatever had happened was so far from him that it had never been so close to him. The grass surged and there was so much truth in that sound, so much boldness. Standing on the far end of the field, Mickey could not be distinguished from the bark of the only tree, he was leaning against the trunk, his eyes were closed, the muscles in his face, like gentle asters, quavered with peaceful anxiety. His pale shadow gladly slid and painlessly cut Mickey's body in half. When Mickey opened his eyes, he saw a little bird in front of him hopping softly like the air at dawn;

hello

hello

The familiar wind blew and cut the guy's peaceful voice. The dandelions sprawled in the grass shook from the broad swings of air. The wind's vigor was nice, its coldness was snowy. The wind might betray their meeting, take the silhouettes and, driving them away like an unexpected apparition, reveal them, even though for that the current of the wind would have to be mighty, it would have to conquer all of the obstacles made of the tree trunks and foliage. But the wind merely gently reminded him and blew only once, as if it were one flap of a bird that had come a long way and had lost its strength and had weakened.

did you bring it?
i brought it

Mickey put his hand to his chest and from his pocket took out the half-crumpled photograph. The gray gloves got a little in the way, but he managed to carefully hold it by its edges with his fingers and, extending his hand, hold it in front of his eyes. On the photograph there were white cracks and miniature scratches, the dog ears at the bottom were cut off, scattered all over the girl's forehead and cheeks were popped bubbles that, as it were, looked like field mushrooms. The only thing that had been salvaged was her naughtily raised bare shoulder; on her shoulder smiled the little flower of her childhood viral vaccine.

three

I am 28 years old. The second perfect number. Every morning, like my grandfather, I ate one banana and drank one cup of coffee. I'm not smart, even though I've read V. S. Naipaul's correspondence with his father, seen André Breton's *Nadja*, studied Deleuze and Guattari's collaborative writings, the works of anonymous illuminators, ridden a bicycle, and drank mulled wine. But everything has changed. Every hour I eat two spoons of washing powder and I wait for Darzukmakhus to play chess with. Darzukmakhus is a bald doll with gouged-out eyes that only wakes up when I swallow the powder and then, when I lie in bed, I think about the next trip of sadness that awaits me in the dark. I'm wearing my grandfather's worn woollen fur coat, I'm standing in front of a mirror, and with my right hand, like Albrecht Dürer, I'm trying to gently bring together the lapels of the coat. You are standing in the mirror completely naked with a long, very long, pitiful fur coat thrown over your shoulders. He is so thin that it seems as if his skin was cooked for a few hours in a pot. Bones like crooked wires; an unarmed skeleton returning home from the battlefield centuries ago; he imagines facial features, eyes, a nose, a mouth, a forehead, tissues, tendons, lungs, a liver. They are divided shadows— icicles—with tousled hair standing on end. Bird's tail sways from side to side and rubs against his legs; it's purring, it's probably hungry. Life to you has always seemed more interesting after death than until death, because life exempts presence, and presence in itself is uninteresting if you don't create it or destroy it down to the ground. It's probably written somewhere or said by someone. The written word and the spoken utterance must be repeated. Repetition never repeats itself. I will never be repeated, merely once. One, two, three, and there, there's a knock on the window. You turn around. It's the little banana. It's waiting. You hug Bird, kiss its nose, take out of your coat pocket a rubber mouse with its ear bitten off, and throw it in front of it. With crazy eyes, the cat jumps on the mouse and starts playing with it. He bends over and pets the cat's back. Goodbye, Bird. Goodbye, you're going, you're going, you're going to say goodbye to your friend, to go, you're going, see? You open the window and look down. There are no children, lively children with pudgy hands. With the fingers of your right hand you gently hold the lapels of Dürer's fur coat;

The street is the same infantry square; even when you're walking at night you have to take your hands out of your pockets, stretch your body, and walk alertly, the chief of headquarters could be in the vicinity, and even without that, your hands in your pants pockets doesn't suit you somehow from the side; your pockets are very deep, your hands practically drown to your elbows in the pockets. With your thumb and index finger, you feel the sunflower seed that you bought from the little pirate and leave it in your pocket. And, aha, it looks like you're at the market, because your body and consciousness start to pleasantly oppress the stacked crates of various sizes to the left and right, the dishes, the pots: the bright, swaying waves of color. Each crate has its own unique look in depth, width, shapelessness. The crooked nails in the blackened slats of the crates that over the course of years have become more and more deeply embedded in the pulp of the wood, imprinting boomerang-like rusty blotches. The papers laid out like bed sheets under the fruits are milky pink here and there with soft hues from the juices that have streamed out of the sour cherries, the strawberries, the raspberries; crumpled newspapers with blurred letters; your eyes like to scrutinize the texts of those cream-colored papers laid under the fruits, at times probing a black-and-white photograph and singling out any kind of text. You try to read some short-lived news, an interesting murder report, an ad: "Persian kitten for sale for 50____, possibility to trade for a piano." Wonderful trade, but why for a piano? Who still plays piano these days? There is danger in coming into the bright world for little kids with bow ties; no one now is born with a bow tie and no one drowns in mazut wearing a bow tie. You reread the ad: Persian kitten for sale for 50___, the rest of the numbers and letters cannot be read with any effort. The drops of water sprinkled on the peels of apples have turned the letters and numbers into thick, inky blots. You come to the marketplace every day to buy fruit, and you always buy not by the kilo, but by the fruit; two oranges, three peaches, one mandarin, definitely two bananas, one to eat on the street, the other with coffee in the morning. To the familiar and the unfamiliar, after the second word, you suddenly admit how important it is to buy fruit every day and take the fruit back to your room immediately from the marketplace, how important it is for human life to have a familiar fruit-seller and how sad his absence is. After a long silence followed by a hysterical chuckle, a wave of uncontrollable laughter rises; fruit-eating beaver, you're not stupid, are you? You're totally dumb, a flamboyant rodent; hahahahahahahahahaha, the laughter is so explosive and lasting that in the end you don't understand whether you guys are laughing or lowing, inside of you, moment after moment, anxiety grows: who's laughing now, where did those frightening, ear-piercing roars resound from?

When you guys get serious, wiping the tearful waters streaming out of your eye sockets with your sleeves or handkerchiefs, you hardly hold in the desire to ask, in actuality, who was laughing half a minute ago and what were they laughing about, did they feel the laughter? You put your head on Bird's soft belly who's sleeping on your pillow, and you quietly give yourself to the passing course of its belly's rhythmic beats; mandarins, oranges, lemons, fibrous kiwis, long-tressed coconuts, *sujukh*[13] hanging at the gallows, Golden Delicious apples with dots and thick peels from the African harvest, rolls of sour lavash, banana bunches, tropical fruits spiky like a hedgehog that are still unrecognizable to your palate, mangos, striped watermelon, mellifluous dried fruit—plum, peach, cherry—unforgettable names, colors, tastes, uninviting sights; dreams about fruits and fruit crates: the most pleasant letters from your father coming from that war zone, in which ripe pears were stacked up layer upon layer. Not finding him among the pears in the crate, you would take one big pear, run to the street, and in front of the open mouths and frozen gazes of your friends, you would eat it with gusto until the very end, and at that moment no one was laughing. You personally know all the unsold fruits and they personally know you. The noticeable smattering of openings in the crates every day look like tiny dry lakes. You remember all the sold fruits, imagining the facial features of the buyers and the furniture of their apartments. On the peel of the apple in the top right corner of the hemp-colored crate there are two bite marks, two small, sharp tears by milk teeth. The white fruit pulp visible through the cracks has turned dark

---

13   *Sujukh* is a thread of walnuts wrapped in hardened plum or apricot syrup. It is usually hung by a thread to dry.

from exposure to the air. That apple is the most delicious, yes, believe it, the most delicious, seriously, because a child bit into it, my grandfather said, asking the buyer to absolutely put that apple in the bag with the rest. You walk up to the corner of the familiar fruit-seller. Pressing against the crate of pineapples is a long metal pole whose twisted kinks hang over the banana bunches. A tall woman, her shoulder leaning against the pole, is staring at your shoes. In the beginning she recognizes you merely by looking at your shoes. It's the woman fruit-seller you've known for years—Nara—formerly an Armenian language teacher. Noticing your familiar shadow from a distance, she gets sort of emotional and, with a sharp-cornered smile on her face, she starts to shake her head erratically. You look at her glaucous, bluish plum-like long face; not a crease; not a wrinkle; it's as if the cold wind has smoothed out her entire skin; her nose: arched, pointing to the sky; her mouth: wide; instead of lips, there are two pale lines; her chin is twisted, hairless; you don't know why in the end all that remains visible are her eyes without eyebrows set in deep sockets with turquoise irises swimming in the whites. You think that maybe these types of facial features shape only the repetitive day-to-day in life, the unique events, and the primitive emotions, as well as the things that constantly surround the body, the not marrying and the drinking of coffee alone. She greets you with her fingers. The tips are cold and weak.

hello

hello

She smiles without looking into your eyes, restlessly stroking the fur collars of your warm military overcoat. He begins to shake his head with a type of rhythmic, systematic flinch. Her ink-colored tongue sticks out of her lips every now and again, licking the edge of her mouth. You're not cold without a jacket? No, I came to say goodbye to you. Her smile widens even more, the corners of her mouth twitch, she begins to carelessly squash the rotten banana peel on the ground. Watching her face for a long time, it seems for a moment that she's no longer smiling, but that she's deliberately contracting all the muscles in her face. Every day he comes to say goodbye. But where are you going? He falls silent. He seriously tilts his head, gnawing his lips with his canines. There's no business today. No one needs softness. You come everyday and say you're leaving, every day you say goodbye to me; are they taking you to the army again? Five years ago they were also taking you to the army, but five years ago you left and didn't come back for a long time, I see you every day, eh, I see you, how do you buy two yellow banan- as from me, because what if I weren't here? Suddenly she begins to laugh somewhat embarrassed, but on the inside with an angry strain. That laugh is like a whole bunch of different chil- dren's voices, disconnected from each other in a disorderly way. Dumpling will miss you. Yeah, how will you buy bananas there? Don't know, I'll ask someone to let me come to the marketplace at least once a week, I sent you a letter by e-mail, you didn't read it? No, I haven't checked my e-mail for ages; I'll definitely check, I'll reply to your letter. Nara's cheeks take on the color of fresh blood and undulate with every uttered word. She has put the tip of her ink-colored tongue under her canine and is squeezing it. But, seriously, are you really going this time? Yeah, I'm going, I can't not go anymore. She promptly collects the banana bunches with care from the kinks of the pole, then arranges them in the crate. Holding the crate with her giant hands, she walks to the neighboring fruit-seller's booth on the opposite side, exchanges a few words with the owner of the booth smoking by the door, and goes in. Some time passes. Nara doesn't come out of the booth. She's probably putting away the crate, you think. The booth owner lights up another cigarette and, with a stupid gaze, follows the flapping of arms of an elderly woman who looks like a turkey and who is vexedly trying to convey some sort of dissatisfaction. You take a deep breath, then you round your mouth and exhale, following the vanishing trail of vapor coming out of you. It's as if your body has been coated with a layer of ice and that layer is protecting you somehow. Nara is running extremely late. You walk to the booth and enter through the half-open door. She's sitting on the floor, in a dark corner, she's holding her head in her hands and softly crooning a song. You tense up, you try to catch and understand the lyrics of the song, but the sound is so weak that no amount of effort helps you discern and understand. You go up to her.

hello

hello

I didn't think you'd come, when I didn't come out of the booth for a long time, I thought you'd come, you wouldn't come, but you came, I stubbornly wouldn't come out, ehhh. She hums the song again. The beautiful, almost skinless fingers of her hands have the color of soil; her cuticles have turned black. Nara's gray woollen hat is visible through her fingers. She's no longer shaking her head. When the song pauses for a moment, the sound of dripping water becomes audible in the deep silence, as if raindrops were dripping one by one on a tin roof. A puddle has formed between Nara's legs. I really like to go inside a place and not come out. Go inside some place and wait for someone to come. When I was little, I would hide in the closet, I would crawl under the bed, but I would dream that they find me, that's why I hid, I got pleasure out of my parents' suffering from having lost me. You waited and waited, you saw that I'm running late, that I'm not coming, you got worried and came, right? You don't say anything. You're generally incapable of talking. When you talk, you always feel sharp pains in different parts of your body. The place where you're going, are there resellers of bananas there? No, besides you, there are no other banana resellers in the world. You both laugh. Listen, what are you going to eat? You'll be hungry on the way, you can't get full on bananas alone, oh, I know, fine, you won't stay hungry; so, you'll probably go by bus, you'll take my baked *gata*[14] with you and eat it, you still have it, right, you remember when I gave it to you? Yeah, I remember. You impulsively put your hand in your pants pocket; you don't find anything other than the sunflower seed. You squeeze it with your thumb and index finger, breaking the seed's dry shell. Sparrows probably pecked at the crumbs of Nara's *gata* and now, one year later, on the same street, you won't find a single trace of crumb. Nara turns around, puts her hand in the crate behind her, breaks off two bananas, and puts them by your feet. Don't forget to take the *gata*, the *gata* I baked, so you can eat it on the bus, so you go and eat it, so the bus goes, takes you, my *gata*; you kept it, didn't you? Yeah, I've kept it; I'll take it with me. Last year; the same two bananas, the same military overcoat, and her embarrassed murmur, I'm free in the evening, come to my house, I've set a table for

---

14   *Gata* is a sweet Armenian pastry.

you; then, practically going into your mouth, she adds, I'm drinking *oghi*. You have a hard time finding the building, you open your notebook at every step, and like a schoolboy reciting poetry you read the address out loud to passers-by you run into in the street. Instead of a wooden, twisted doorknob, it's a round black hole stuffed with a piece of sponge. You take your notebook out of your coat pocket, leaf through it, find the corresponding page, and read: knock on the door twice. You tear out that page, put it in your mouth, and start to chew it, continually wetting it with your tongue and turning it over in different corners of your mouth. After properly chewing up the paper, you swallow it, then, taking a deep breath, you knock on the door: one, two. Some sort of sounds are audible from the inside, as if they were the dry blows of a hammer. Nara lives by herself. She told me many times that she got married once in her life, that her husband's mother had them divorce because of her infertility, then her husband married a second time and is now the father of two children; he lives with his family in the building next door. Nara says that she and her ex-husband frequently meet in the street and she always asks her ex-husband: did you know that I also have child? No one knows that I also have a child, but I also have a child, a girl, Italians cured me, they took out my uterus and put an Italian uterus in its place. You believe Nara and every now and again you imagine her Italian uterus: decorated with little birds just like on yellow, green, red balloons, and in one of which her girl is sleeping. The door half-opens when you are getting ready to leave. Like a frightened animal, Nara peeks through the door, her irises twirl with the speed of a maniac in the whites of her eyes. She fixes her gaze now on your face, now on your shoes, your face, your shoes, your face, as if convincing herself that the shoes you are wearing are the ones she saw. Your face for her is your shoes. Opening the door more widely before long, she greets with two fingers and, erratically skipping back and forth like a goat, she suddenly disappears. You have frozen undecidedly in front of the open door, you don't know whether to go in now or wait. The smell of old suitcases wafts from the apartment. The darkness of the narrow hall is so dense that it blocks any light coming through. You think you'll probably wait a long time. Maybe she went to the bathroom. To keep busy, you take out your notebook again, leaf through it, and read:

Have heard the splash, the forsaken cry,
But for him it was not an important failure; the sun shone
As it had to on the white legs disappearing into the green
Water, and the expensive delicate ship that must have seen
Something amazing, a boy falling out of the sky,
Had somewhere to get to and sailed calmly on.

(W. H. Auden, "Musée des Beaux Arts")

Had somewhere to get to and sailed calmly on; sailed calmly on, sailed calmly on; You turn to the last lines and remember the way: the tortuous water path leading in deep silence to the sea flanked on both sides with trees with high branches and snow-white leaves; Come in. Nara's voice was so unfamiliar and faint that for a moment it seemed to you as if those words were releasing themselves from the mouth of some dying patient lying inside. If there's a dying patient in the apartment, you will leave right now, because you cannot understand any bedridden patients in the world. Nara lives by herself. Years ago, when they had first met, sober, she had told him all the details, that her mother had passed away long ago, during those bad years.[15] She died suddenly when they were drinking coffee in the morning. She was sitting across from her. After the second sip, when she put the cup down, her eyes glistened with different colors like the eyes of a cat, and they had become a little moist. She no longer said anything. She held the ear of the cup with her finger and thumb. I leaned over and looked into her cup, she had only drank half of it, I asked: you don't like it? She didn't say anything; she only smiled. She smiled very widely. Her wrinkles practically rubbed against her ear lobes. I had never seen such a candid and happy smile on her face. In the beginning it seemed as if she were smiling at me, because her gaze was directed at my face, but the missing concreteness in her eyes and the monotony of her gaze turned her vision out of focus without a sign, it seemed as if she were now looking through her left eye, now through her forehead, now through her nose, now through her mouth. When I got out of my chair, taking my cup from the table, she was still smiling, but this time at the rails of the chair. I was teaching morning classes at school. I got dressed, picked up my bag, and, not going into the living room, I told my mother that I'd bring bread with me and reminded her not to forget her blood pressure medication. She didn't say anything. I locked the door with a key and went out. After classes, I went to stand in line

---

15   The "bad years" refer to the years following Armenia's independence from the Soviet Union in 1991. An entire system had collapsed, Armenia was still suffering from the aftermath of a devastating earthquake in 1988, and the army was fighting a war against Azerbaijan over Nagorno-Karabakh. All these factors led to approximately five years of extreme poverty, hunger, and cold. Colloquially, these years, spanning from 1991 to 1996, are known as the "bad years" or "dark years."

for bread. It was getting dark when my turn came and I rushed home with the bread in my hands. As always, to not worry my mother, I opened the door with a key. It was colder than usual inside and it seemed to me that I had left a window open. A sort of sweet-rotten smell had spread through the house. The smell was foreign. My heart started to beat fast. I wasn't moving forward. I called my mother. She didn't answer. I started to slowly walk towards the door of the living room. Her thick back was visible through the wide-open door. She was sitting at the table in the same position. I stood in the doorway and I looked at her back for a long time. For a moment I confused the beats of my heart with the ticks of the clock on the wall, but then I remembered that the batteries of the clock didn't work and that the hands had frozen a long time ago. I asked, what are you doing, mom? She didn't say anything. I slowly walked up to her back. When I wanted to put my hand on her shoulder, I suddenly regretted it; I turned around, closed my eyes, and sat across from her on the chair I had sat on before. With my eyes closed, I called her again: mom. A cold current of air blew in my face, and I strongly felt the sweet-rotten smell. I opened my eyes. The wide smile frozen on my mother's face since morning hit me in the face like a ball. Saliva thin as the thread on a spindle hung from the corners of her mouth. She was still holding the ear of the coffee cup with her finger and thumb. I jumped up and pushed her shoulder as hard as I could with my hand. She tipped over on her back together with the chair. Her face shook from her body hitting the floor. It was as if a giant statue, weighing a few tons, crumbled. I sat in my chair. For almost an hour I was looking at her coffee cup and foot sticking up in the air by the edge of the table. Some time later I called her again: mom! She didn't answer. She's died, I thought and went out of the house to call a neighbor.

Nara is standing by the living room door, from where she had seen her mother's thick back. Maybe her mother is sitting at the table, you think. Nara has her head hanging down. Waving her hand behind her, she invites me in. You enter the living room. Suddenly your eyes are struck by the table and the two wooden chairs set across from each other. There's no mother. Nara wasn't lying. You begin to shiver horribly. It was warmer outside than inside. The cold, drifting waves make your face twitch by itself. The living room doesn't have parquet flooring. There is missing wallpaper here and there. On the metal bed leaning against the wall, there are dirty rags, sooty pajamas, and piles of bras with a stereo placed on top of them. By the window is Nara's desk, on top of which there is an old computer model with a big screen surrounded by books and notebooks. There seems to be nothing else in the living room. You can sit down, she says without raising her head and pointing with her hand at the chair by the table. You walk to the chair and sit at the table, take out the *oghi* from your coat pocket, and put it on the table. Your lowered eyes rise by themselves, open up and stare at the empty chair in front of you. You begin to intently examine the wooden chair. You can't see Nara's mother in any way. The chair is empty. After looking for a long time, for a moment it seems as if the chair is smiling; it's smiling with the same wide smile as Nara's mother. A shudder runs through your body. Clenching your hands into fists, you put them in your coat pockets, and dig your head deeper into its sharp-edged lapels. She is standing next to you. You look at the grey concrete and you're convinced that Nara is also looking at the grey concrete. Then you look at the transparent bottle of *oghi* and you're convinced that right at that same moment Nara is also looking at the transparent bottle of *oghi*. I'll be back in a sec, she says. You hear the sound of falling plates coming out of the kitchen. She soon brings juice glasses and clanks them on the table one by one. You can open the *oghi*. I'll bring pastry now. You take off the cap of the bottle and fill the glasses. She comes back with a huge soup plate in her hand. She approaches you with slow, almost official, steps. She puts the plate in front of you. In the big soup plate was a little frosted *gata*. I worked on it very hard all day yesterday, she says. I got out of the marketplace an hour earlier to bake this for you. The gata's pale crust and thin white little layer of dough sadly look at your face. The *gata* is so delicate that for an instance it takes you an incredible amount of effort to notice it in the big plate. Sorry, I don't have a knife for cutting pastry. I don't want any. I made it for you. Have it all. Sure, hang on, I'll be back in a sec. Once again she quickly goes to the kitchen and comes back, this time bringing a doll with her. Meet Dumpling.

Sayhellodumplinghowareyoudumplingseei'vecometoeatp astry. You fall silent. She lays down the doll, putting its head on the edge of the plate. One of the arms of the doll is missing and its face is scribbled with a blue pen. You make yourself comfortable, I'll stand, I'll look at you and Dumpling from above. Want to drink? Yeah, let's drink. Nara grabs the glass joyously screeching wheeeeeeeeeeeeeeeeeeeeeeee. We're drinking without cheers. I'm a vegetarian, she suddenly says. You fill the empty glasses again. Nara continues. Vegetarianism prolongs a person's life. We pick up the glasses and quaff them down. I want to break the record of longest lifespan. Now and again she holds the neck of the doll with two fingers, pushes its head into the *gata*, and makes it peck: you don't want to eat *gata*, huh, you don't want it either, huh, you don't want *gata*, huh, I baked it for you, why don't you want it, my *gata*'s not good, huh? But I made it well. I eat one carrot a day to keep my blood running. I got dismissed from school, but, if I live long, they'll take me back. I always put glasses on the window sill and collect rainwater. Every Friday I drink, I knock on wood three times and drink one glass of rainwater for my bones, so they don't wear when I age, so they don't break. If I break my leg, there won't be anyone to take care of me, I'll starve, I won't be able to go to the marketplace. I eat dates so that my brain functions well, so that I don't get tired easily, so that I read a lot, so that if they take me back to work, I work well with my kids. Once in a while, say, once every three months, I take a shower, I don't shower much so that the bacteria don't bite my skin. I don't eat meat at all. If I weren't going to live long, I'd eat it. The doll doesn't make a sound. You fill the glasses. The bottle empties. You drink looking at the little *gata* lying in the plate. How beautiful you are, little *gata*. I'll be back in a sec, Nara says again and, stumbling from drunkenness, she walked out of the living room with her arms spread wide. Your head is spinning. You're numb. You feel tired. Suddenly your shoulder sways with Nara's dry shakes. You turn around. From her waist down, she is completely naked. She has pulled her pants and panties down to her knees. There are small red fish on Nara's yellow panties. She laughed and continued to vigorously shake your shoulder. You get out of your chair and stand in front of her. She practically bangs your head against her belly. A little below is the Italian uterus. Nara is smiling from above, as if she were a Greek goddess. Frightened, like a puppy dog, she starts to stroke your spiky hair with four fingers. You try to bend over, to pull up her panties, but she pulls away. I eat two bunches of herbs a day to die at 130, wheeeeeeeeeeeee, tango, Nara shrieks clapping her hands, let's tango; now, right now, let's dance. Without pulling up her pants and panties, she shuffles up to the stereo, tosses her clothes and rags aside, finds a black tape lost under some dust, places it in the cassette deck without a holder, and turns on the stereo. After some piercing crackles, a melody becomes audible. Nara shuffles up to you. You bend over again, you try to pull up her panties and pants, she grasps your hand: leave it, please. Nara's entreatment sounds so soft and gentle that you instinctively raise your hands and embrace her back.

Sentolambadaey sentolambadaey sentolambadaey sentolambadaey; let's dance slow, slow, Nara says. You lightly move your bodies. Nara's leans to the right, you lean to the left, she leans to the left, you lean to the right; sentolambadaey, sentolambadaey, sentolambadaey. You begin to turn in the empty room, you turn, turn, turn, you've put your head on Nara's Italian uterus and try to listen to the chirps of the decorated colorful little birds and the throbs of her little girl's heart sentolambadaaaaaaaaaaaaaaaaaaaa, you turn, turn, turn, turn, turn, turn, turn, turn, sento, s en t ooooo; unable to maintain your balance, you fall on the floor, you to one side, Nara to the other. The song has ended. You can hear the piercing tape, the creaking of the turning engine, and an endless crackle. You both gasp. I, I da-dance very, very badly. I dance to this heeeeey tango every day with Dumpling, I'm preparing Dumpling for the wedding tango, sentoooooooooooooolambadaaaaaaaaaeeeeeeeeeeey, Nara screams. An oval drop of sweat glistens on her temple. You get up with great difficulty and slowly walk to the door. We're going to live for a thousand years, we're going to live for so long, it'll be just us in the end, no, we're going to live for three thousand years, that's why I grind banana peels, stir them in water, and drink them, to not get a heart attack or stroke. Say it, too, say that we'll live for a thousand years, come on, say it, say it; or come, let's say it together. Three oooh four: we're going to live for three thousand years. Looooong liiiiiiiive uuuuuuuus, Nara laughs. You've already reached the door; with your finger, you take out the piece of sponge stuffed in the hole of the missing doorknob, you pull it towards you with your index finger, and open the door. You don't want to have some *gata*, huh, you don't want it either, huh, you don't want to have some *gata*, huh, nice *gata*, I made it, no one wants it, no one wants my *gata*, no one, you don't want it either, huh? The doll doesn't say anything. You hear shuffling. She's coming to see you off. Shuffleshuffleshuffle. She's behind you. You're already in the doorway. At the moment of goodbye, you turn to her. The pants lost in dust. The yellow panties with little red fish. Trembling, scaly legs. The military overcoat; you go up, up, and suddenly it's as if you were seeing Nara for the first time in your life. She's smiling with a wide very wide smile, at peace and happy. Her eyes are shining. She looks your way without blinking. Then, not moving the direction of her gaze by even one inch, she extends her open palm to you; in it, there's the little *gata* wrapped in a tissue. You take the *gata*, put it in your hand, and ceremoniously holding your hand up in the air, you go down the stairs. For a moment you stop and strain your ears. Nara closes the door, gently. You continue to go down, holding your hand up in the air. You come out to the street. The sleet has whitened the weeds that have grown through the granite edges of the sidewalks. It's getting dark. You cross the intersection and stand by the tree, you lean one hand against the gray trunk, carefully put the *gata* on the ground, take off your winter shoes one after another, throw them under the trunk, then you hug the tree with both hands and put your head on the bark. Soon you put the *gata* back in your hand, you emphatically extend your hand in front of you and continue to walk. The air is pleasant, mood-enhancing, you work on cutting and passing by all the big and small seas you encounter: you're skipping. The streams of water sprinkle in the air and fall on your shoulders. You start to dance, dance, sentoooooooooooooo, you scream and walk to the next sea, to the next, next sea, to the next next next sea, to the next, next, next sea.

2009-2010, 2011-2012